"I *want* the world to know that I am the father. You have my child in your belly, Lisa. Do you really think I intend to relinquish my claim on my own flesh and blood?"

The words sounded almost *primitive* and they were filled with a sense of possession. They reminded Lisa of the full force of Luc's power and the fact that he had grown up with very different values to her. "Of course I don't!" she said. "We can meet with a lawyer and have a legal agreement drawn up. You can see your child anytime you like—within reason. Surely you can have no objection to that?"

His eyes were cold and so was his voice. "I think you are missing the point, *cherie*. I intend to marry you."

"I'm sorry, Luc." She gave a slight shake of her head as she reached for the door handle. "I'm afraid that's just not going to happen."

"I don't want to have to fight you to get what I want, Lisa," he said softly as they reached her door. "But if you force my hand then I'm afraid that's what's going to happen. Perhaps I should warn you now that it is better not to defy me."

D1021779

One Night With Consequences

When one night...leads to pregnancy!

When succumbing to a night of unbridled desire, it's impossible to think past the morning after!

But, with the sheets barely settled, that little blue line appears on the pregnancy test, and it doesn't take long to realize that one night of white-hot passion has turned into a lifetime of consequences!

Only one question remains:

How do you tell a man you've just met that you're about to share more than just his bed?

Find out in:

Look for more **One Night With Consequences** stories coming soon!

Sharon Kendrick

CROWNED FOR THE PRINCE'S HEIR

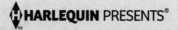

If you purchased this book without a cover you should be aware that this book is stolen property. It was reported as "unsold and destroyed" to the publisher, and neither the author nor the publisher has received any payment for this "stripped book."

Recycling programs
for this product may
not exist in your area.

ISBN-13: 978-0-373-13458-8

Crowned for the Prince's Heir

First North American Publication 2016

Copyright © 2016 by Sharon Kendrick

All rights reserved. Except for use in any review, the reproduction or utilization of this work in whole or in part in any form by any electronic, mechanical or other means, now known or hereinafter invented, including xerography, photocopying and recording, or in any information storage or retrieval system, is forbidden without the written permission of the publisher, Harlequin Enterprises Limited, 225 Duncan Mill Road, Don Mills, Ontario M3B 3K9, Canada.

This is a work of fiction. Names, characters, places and incidents are either the product of the author's imagination or are used fictitiously, and any resemblance to actual persons, living or dead, business establishments, events or locales is entirely coincidental.

This edition published by arrangement with Harlequin Books S.A.

For questions and comments about the quality of this book, please contact us at CustomerService@Harlequin.com.

® and TM are trademarks of Harlequin Enterprises Limited or its corporate affiliates. Trademarks indicated with ® are registered in the United States Patent and Trademark Office, the Canadian Intellectual Property Office and in other countries.

Printed in U.S.A.

Sharon Kendrick once won a national writing competition by describing her ideal date: being flown to an exotic island by a gorgeous and powerful man. Little did she realize that she'd just wandered into her dream job! Today she writes for Harlequin, featuring often stubborn but always *to die for* heroes and the women who bring them to their knees. She believes that the best books are those you never want to end. Just like life...

Books by Sharon Kendrick

Harlequin Presents

The Ruthless Greek's Return
Christmas in Da Conti's Bed
The Greek's Marriage Bargain
A Scandal, a Secret, a Baby
The Sheikh's Undoing
Monarch of the Sands
Too Proud to Be Bought

The Bond of Billionaires

Claimed for Makarov's Baby
The Sheikh's Christmas Conquest

One Night With Consequences

Carrying the Greek's Heir

Desert Men of Qurhah

Defiant in the Desert
Shamed in the Sands
Seduced by the Sultan

Wedlocked!

The Billionaire's Defiant Acquisition

Visit the Author Profile page at Harlequin.com for more titles.

With special thanks to a dear friend—the wildly talented and inspirational Stewart Parvin—who designs amazing clothes and wedding dresses for discerning royals and women everywhere!

CHAPTER ONE

THE NAME LOOMED up in front of him and on the back seat of the limousine, Luc's powerful body tensed. He knew what he ought to do. Ignore it. Drive on without a backward glance. Forget the past and accept the future which was waiting for him. But the dark voice of his conscience was forgotten as he leaned forward to speak to his driver, because sometimes curiosity was just too damned strong to resist.

'Stop the car,' he ordered harshly.

The car slid to a halt in the quiet street of London's Belgravia, a street full of unusual restaurants and tasteful shops. But only one of these caught his eye—which was surprising, since Luciano wasn't the kind of man who had ever featured shopping as a hobby. He didn't need to. Even the expensive baubles discreetly bought as compensatory keepsakes for departing lovers were purchased on his behalf by one of his many staff.

But there had been no purchase of baubles for quite a while now and no heartbroken lovers to pacify. He had recently undertaken two long years of celibacy—not exactly happily, but because he'd recognised it was something he needed to do. And he had risen to the challenge. His mouth hardened at the unintended pun. He had channelled his considerable energies into his work. He had worn out his hard body with exercise. His mind had been clear, strong and focussed—yet he wondered where that focus was now as he read the two words scrolled in fancy letters above the shop across the street.

Lisa Bailey.

He could feel the sudden throbbing of his groin as her name whispered into his memory just as her soft voice had once whispered urgent little entreaties into his ear as he drove deep inside her. Lisa Bailey. The hottest lover he'd ever known. The talented designer with the unblinking gaze. The tumble-haired temptress with the delicious curves.

And the only woman to kick him out of her bed.

Luc shifted in his seat, locked in an uncharacteristic moment of indecision because ex-lovers had the potential to be complicated—and complications he didn't need right now. He should tap on the glass and tell his chauffeur to drive on. Continue the journey to his embassy and deal with any last-minute queries before he returned to his island home after the wedding. He thought about what awaited him in Mardovia, and a sudden stillness settled over him. He had a duty to fulfil, or a burden to carry. It all depended which way you looked at it, and if he preferred to look for the positive rather than the negative—who could blame him?

His gaze returned to the shop front, and it was then that he saw her walking across the showroom and the pounding in his heart increased as he glimpsed the tumble of her curls. She turned slightly—showcasing the swell of her magnificent breasts. Lust arrowed sharply down into his groin, and stayed there.

Lisa Bailey.

His eyes narrowed. It was strange to see her here in this expensive part of town—far away from the edgier area of London where their paths had first crossed, in the tiny studio where she had designed her dresses.

He told himself it didn't matter why she was here because he didn't care. *Yet he was the one who had directed his driver to take this route, wasn't he?* And all because he'd heard some woman mention her name and had discovered that Lisa Bailey had come up in the world. His tongue snaked out over suddenly dry lips. What harm could it do to drop in and say hello, for old times' sake? Wasn't that what ex-lovers did? And wouldn't it convince him—as if he needed any convincing—that he was over her?

'Wait down the road a little,' he told the driver, opening the door himself and stepping onto the pavement. A few discreet yards away, a second car containing his bodyguards had also stopped, but Luc gave an almost imperceptible signal to tell them to keep their distance.

The August sun was hot on his head and there wasn't a whisper of wind in the leaves of the trees in the nearby square, despite the fact that it was getting on for five o'clock. The city had been caught up in a heatwave so fierce that news bulletins had been featuring clips of people frying eggs on the pavement and lying sprawled in the city's parks in various states of undress. Luc was looking forward to getting back to the air-conditioned cool of his palace in Mardovia. There white doves cooed in the famous gardens and the scent of the roses was far sweeter than the clogging traffic fumes which surrounded him here in the city. If it hadn't been for Conall Devlin's wedding party this weekend then he might have taken an earlier flight. Back to begin the process of embracing his new future—which he intended to do with whole-hearted dedication.

He pushed open the shop door and there she was, crouched down beside a rail of dresses with a needle in her hand and a tape measure around her neck—worn in the same way as a doctor might wear a stethoscope.

'Hello, Lisa,' he said, his tongue curling around the words as once it had curled around the soft swell of her breasts.

Lisa glanced up and narrowed her eyes against the light and at first she didn't recognise him. Maybe because he was the last person she was expecting to see, or maybe because she was tired and it was the end of a long day. A hot day at the end of August, with most people away on holiday and the city overrun by tourists who weren't really interested in buying the kind of clothes she was selling.

She felt the clench of rising hope as the doorbell gave its silvery little tinkle and a tall figure momentarily blotted out the blaze of the summer sun as the man stepped inside. She was due to close soon—but what did that matter? If this was a customer then he could stay until midnight for all she cared! She would switch on her best smile and persuade him to buy an armful of silk dresses for his wife. As he moved towards her she got an overwhelming impression of power and sensuality, and she tried to keep the cynicism from her smile as it crossed her mind that a man like this was more likely to be buying for his mistress than his wife.

But then he said her name and she stiffened because nobody else had an accent quite like his.

She could feel the painful squeeze of her heart and the sudden rush of heat to her breasts. The needle she was holding fell to the carpet and vaguely she found herself thinking that she *never* dropped a needle. But then the thought was gone and the only one left dominating her mind was the fact that Luc was standing in her shop. His full name was Prince Luciano Gabriel Leonidas—head of the ancient royal House of Sorrenzo and ruler of the island principality of Mardovia.

But Lisa hadn't cared that he'd been a prince. She had known him simply as Luc. The man who had—unbelievably—become her lover. Who had introduced her to physical bliss and shown her that it had no limits. He'd made her feel things she'd never believed herself capable of feeling. Things she hadn't *wanted* to feel if the truth was known— because with desire came fear. Fear of being hurt. Fear of being let down and betrayed as women so often were—and that had scared the life out of her. He'd told her he wasn't looking for love or commitment and that had suited her just fine until she'd started to care for him.

She'd done her best to hide her growing feelings and had succeeded, until the day she'd realised she was fighting a losing battle with her heart. And that was when common sense had intervened and she had shrunk away from him—like someone picking up a pan to discover that the handle was burning hot. Telling him it was over hadn't been easy—and neither had the sleepless nights which followed. But it was easier than getting her heart broken and she hadn't once regretted her decision. Because men like Luc were dangerous—it was written into their DNA.

Her gaze flickered over him and immediately she became aware of the powerful sex appeal which surrounded him like an aura. His black hair was shorter than she remembered, but his eyes were just as blue. That brilliant sapphire blue—as inviting as a swimming pool on a hot day. Eyes you just wanted to dive straight into.

As always he looked immaculate. His hand-made Italian suit was creaseless and his silk shirt was unbuttoned at the neck, revealing a tantalising triangle of silken skin. Lisa wished she didn't feel so warm and uncomfortable. That she'd had a chance to brush her wayward curls or slick a little lipstick over lips which suddenly felt like parchment.

'Luc,' she said, and the name sounded so right—even though it was two years since she'd spoken it. Two long years since she'd gasped it out in delight as he'd filled her and her body had splintered into yet another helpless orgasm around his powerful thrust. 'You're…' She swallowed. 'You're the last person I expected to see.'

He closed the shop door behind him and Lisa

glanced over his shoulder, wondering where his bodyguards were. Lurking out of sight, probably. Trying to blend in to the upmarket location by peering into windows, or melting into the dark shadows of a shop doorway as they controlled access to their royal boss. And then she saw two low black cars with tinted windows parked further down the road and she was reminded of all the protocol which surrounded this charismatic man.

'Am I?' he questioned softly.

His voice was velvet and steel and Lisa felt a rush of desire which made her feel momentarily breathless. Against her lace brassiere her nipples hardened and her skin grew tight. She could feel the instant rush of heat to her sex. And it wasn't fair. How did he manage to provoke that kind of reaction with just one look?

So stay calm. Act like he's a customer. Maybe he *was* a customer—eager to commission one of her trademark silk dresses for one of his countless girlfriends. After all, wasn't that how she'd met him, when he'd walked into her workroom near Borough Market and she hadn't had a clue who he was? Her designs had just been taking off— mainly through word of mouth and thanks to a model who had worn one of her dresses to a film premiere. All sorts of people had started coming to see her, so it hadn't been that surprising to see the imposing, raven-haired man with a beautiful blonde model on his arm.

She remembered the blonde trying to draw his attention to one of the embroidered cream gowns Lisa had been making at the time and which women sometimes wore as wedding dresses. And Lisa remembered looking up and witnessing the faint grimace on Luc's face. Somehow she had understood that he was no stranger to the matrimonial intentions of women, and their eyes had met in a shared moment of unwilling complicity until she had looked away, feeling awkward and slightly flustered.

But something had happened in that split second of silent communication. Something she could never entirely understand. He had dumped the blonde soon afterwards and laid siege to Lisa—in a whirlwind of extravagant gestures and sheer determination to get her into his bed. He had turned all that blazing power on her and at first she'd thought she had been dreaming—especially when she'd discovered that he was a prince. But she hadn't been dreaming. The amazing flowers which had started arriving daily at her workshop had borne testament to his wealth and his intentions. Lisa had tried to resist him—knowing she had no place at the side of someone like him. But it had turned out he hadn't really wanted her by his *side*—he'd just wanted her writhing under-

neath him, or on top of him, or pushed up against
a wall by him, and in the end she'd given in. Of
course she had. She would have defied any woman
to have held out against the potent attraction of
the Mediterranean Prince.

They had dated—if you could call it that—for
six weeks. Weeks which had whizzed by in a blur
of sensuality. He'd never taken her to any of the
glitzy functions featured on the stiff cards which
had been stacked on the marble fireplace of his
fancy house, which she had visited only once,
under the cloak of darkness. He had been reluctant to be anywhere which didn't have a nearby
bed, but Lisa hadn't cared. Because during those
weeks he had taught her everything he knew about
sex, which was considerable. She had never experienced anything like it—not before, and certainly not since.

The memory cleared as she realised that he was
standing in her shop, still exuding that beguiling
masculinity which made her want to go right over
there and kiss him. And she couldn't afford to
think that way.

'So you were just passing?' she questioned politely as she bent and picked up her fallen needle.

'Well, not exactly,' he said. 'I heard in a round-
about way that you'd moved premises and was
interested to see how far up in the world you've
come. And it seems like you've come a long way.'

His eyes glittered as he looked around. 'This is quite some change of circumstance, Lisa.'

She smiled. 'I know.'

'So what prompted the transformation from edgy designer to becoming part of the establishment?'

Lisa kept her expression neutral as she met his curious gaze and even though she owed him no explanation, she found herself giving him one anyway. He probably wouldn't leave until she told him and she wanted him to leave, because he was making her feel uncomfortable standing there, dominating her little shop. 'I was selling stuff online and from my workshop—but it was too far out of the city centre to appeal to the kind of women who were buying my clothes.'

'And?'

She shrugged. 'And then when the opportunity came up to lease a shop in this area, I leapt at the chance.' It had been a bad decision of course, although it had taken her a while to see that. She hadn't realised that you should never take out an expensive lease unless you were confident you could meet the charges, and she'd chosen a backer who didn't know a lot about the fashion industry. But she had been buoyed up and swept away on a wave of acclaim for her dresses—and had needed a new project to fill the void left in her heart after Luc had gone. And then when her sister had announced she was going to have a baby, Lisa's desire to increase her income had become less of an ego-boosting career move and more of a necessity...

He was looking around the shop. 'You've done well,' he observed.

'Yes. Very well.' The lie slipped with practised ease from her tongue, but she justified it by telling herself that all she was doing was protecting herself, though she wasn't quite sure from what. And everyone knew that if you talked yourself up, then people might start to believe in you. 'So what can I do for you?' She fixed him with her most dazzling smile. 'You want to buy a dress?'

'No, I don't want to buy a dress.'

'Oh?' She felt the unsteady beat of her heart. 'So?'

He glittered her a smile. 'Why am I here?'

'Well, yes.'

Why indeed? Luc studied her. To prove she meant nothing? That she was just some tousle-haired temptress who had made him unbelievably hot and horny—before she'd shown him the door.

But wasn't that what rankled, even now? That she had walked away without a second glance—despite his expectation that she'd come crawling back to tell him she'd made the biggest mistake of her life. His pride had been wounded in a way it had never been wounded before, because no woman had ever rejected him—and his disbelief had quickly given way to frustration. With Lisa, he felt like a man who'd had his ice cream taken away from him with still half the cone left to lick.

As his gaze roved over her, the sheer individuality of her appearance hit him on a purely visceral level. He had dated some of the world's most desirable women—beautiful women whose endlessly long legs gave him the height he preferred in his sexual partners. But Lisa was not tall. She was small, with deliciously full breasts which drew a man's eyes to them no matter what she was wearing, or however much she tried to disguise them. She was none of the things he usually liked and yet there was something about her which he'd found irresistible, and he still couldn't work out what that something was.

Today she was wearing a simple silk dress of her own design. The leafy colour emphasised the unusual green-gold of her eyes and fell to just above her bare knees. Her long, curly hair was caught in tortoiseshell clips at the sides, presumably in an attempt to tame the corkscrew curls. Yet no amount of taming could disguise the colour of her crowning glory—a rich, shiny caramel which always reminded him of hazelnut shells. A glossy tendril of it had escaped and was lying against her smooth skin.

But then he noticed something else. The dark

shadows which were smudged beneath her eyes and the faint pinching of her lips. She looked like a woman who was short on sleep and long on worry.

Why?

He met question in her eyes. 'I'm often in this part of town and it seemed crazy not to come in and say hello.'

'So now you have.'

'Now I have,' he agreed as his mind took him off on a more dangerous tangent. He found himself remembering the silken texture of her thighs and the way he had trailed slow kisses over them. The rosy flush which used to flower above her breasts as she shuddered out her orgasm. And he wondered why he was torturing himself with memories which had kick-started his libido so that he could barely think straight.

His mouth hardened. Soon his life would follow a predictable pattern which was inevitable if you were born with royal blood. Yet some trace of the man he would never be called out to him now with a siren voice—and that siren's name was Lisa Bailey. For this was the woman who had fulfilled him on almost every level. Who had never imposed her will on him or made demands on him as so many women tried to. Was that why the sex had been so incredible—because she had made him feel so *free*?

And suddenly the self-imposed hunger of his

two celibate years gnawed at his senses. An appetite so long denied now threatened to overwhelm him and he didn't feel inclined to stop it. What harm could there be in one final sweet encounter before he embraced his new life and all the responsibilities which came with it? Wouldn't that rid him of this woman's lingering memory once and for all?

'I've just flown in from the States and I'm here for a party this weekend,' he said. 'And on Monday I leave for Mardovia.'

'This is all very fascinating, Luc,' she observed drily. 'But I fail to see what any of this has to do with me.'

Luc gave a short laugh, for nobody had ever spoken to him as candidly as Lisa—nor regarded him quite so unflinchingly. And wasn't that one of the things which had always intrigued him about her—that she was so damned *enigmatic*? No dramatic stream of emotion ever crossed *her* pale face. Her features were as cool as if they had been carved from marble. The only time that serene look had ever slipped was when he'd been making love to her and it was then that her defences had melted. He'd liked making her scream and call out his name. He'd liked the way she gasped as he drove deep inside her.

He smiled now, enjoying the familiar lick of

sexual *frisson* between them. 'And I thought I might ask you a favour,' he said.

'*Me?*'

'Well, we're old friends, aren't we?' He saw her pupils dilate in surprise and wondered how she would respond if he came right out and told her what was playing in his head.

I want to have sex with you one last time so that I can forget you. I want to bend my lips to those magnificent nipples and lick them until you are squirming. I want to guide myself into your tight heat and ride you until all my passion is spent.

His pulse pounded loudly in his ears. 'And isn't that what old friends do—ask each other favours?' he murmured.

'I guess so,' she said, her voice uncertain, as if she was having trouble associating their relationship with the word *friendship*.

'I need a date,' he explained. 'Someone to take to a fancy wedding with me. Not the ceremony itself—for those I avoid whenever possible—but the evening reception afterwards.'

Now he had a reaction.

'Oh, come on, Luc,' she said quietly. '*You* need a date? You of all people? I can't believe you're re-visiting an old lover when there must be so many new ones out there. There must be women lining up around the block to go out with you—unless something is radically different and you've had a complete personality change.'

He gave an answering smile and wondered what she would say if she knew the truth. 'I cannot deny that there are any number of women who would happily accompany me,' he said. 'But none of them entice me sufficiently enough to take them.'

'So why not go on your own?'

'Unfortunately, it is not quite that simple.' He glanced out of the window, where he could see the shadowy shapes of his bodyguards standing beside one of the waiting limousines. 'If I turn up without a woman, that will leave me in a some-what vulnerable position.'

'You? *Vulnerable?*' She gave a little snort of a laugh. 'You're about as vulnerable as a Siberian tiger!'

'An interesting metaphor,' he mused. 'Since, in my experience, weddings are a prime hunting ground for women.'

'Hunting ground?' she repeated, as if she'd mis-heard him.

'I'm afraid so.' He gave an unapologetic shrug. 'Some women see the bride and want to be her and so they look around to find the most suitable candidate for themselves.'

Her eyebrows arched. 'You being the most suit-able candidate, I suppose?'

Luc looked at the tendril of hair still lying against

her pale cheek and wanted to curl it around his finger. He wanted to use it like a rope and pull her towards him until their lips were mere inches apart. And then he wanted to kiss her. He shifted his weight a little. 'I'm afraid that being a prince does rather put me in that category—certainly amongst some women.'

'But you think you'd be safe with me?'

'Of course I would.' He paused. 'Our relationship was over a long time ago, and even when it was in full swing neither of us was under any illusion that there was any kind of future in it. You were probably the only woman who truly understood that. You can protect me from the inevitable predators.' He smiled. 'And it might be fun to spend the evening together. Because we know each other well enough to be comfortable around each other, don't we, Lisa?'

Lisa looked at him. *Comfortable?* Was he insane? Didn't he realise that her pulse had been hammering like a piston ever since he'd stepped inside the shop? That her breasts were so swollen that it felt as if she'd suddenly gone up a bra size? Slowly, she drew in a deep breath. 'I think it's a bad idea,' she said flatly. 'A very bad idea. And now if you don't mind—I'm about to shut up shop.'

She walked over to the door and turned the sign to *Closed* and it was only afterwards that she wondered if it was that gesture of finality which suddenly prompted him to try a different approach, because Luc was nothing if not persistent. Because suddenly, he began to prowl around the shop like a caged tiger. Walking over to one of the rails, he slowly ran his fingertips along the line of silk dresses, a thoughtful expression on his face as he turned around to look at her.

'Your shop seems remarkably quiet for what should be a busy weekday afternoon,' he observed.

She tried not to look defensive. To replicate the same cool expression he was directing at her. 'And your point is?'

'My point is that a society wedding would provide an excellent opportunity for you to showcase your talent.' His blue eyes glittered. 'There will be plenty of influential people there. You could wear one of your own designs and dazzle the other guests—isn't that how it works? Play your cards right and I'm sure you could pick up a whole lot of new customers.'

And now Lisa really *was* tempted, because business hadn't been great. Actually, that was a bit of an understatement. Business had taken a serious dive, and she wasn't sure if it was down to the dodgy state of the economy or the more frightening possibility that her clothes had simply gone out of fashion. She'd found herself looking gloomily at magazines which featured dresses which looked a lot like hers—only for a quarter of the price. True, most of the cheaper outfits were made from viscose rather than silk, but lately she'd started wondering if women really cared about that sort of thing any more.

She kept telling herself that the dip in her profits was seasonal—a summer slump which would soon pick up with the new autumn collection, and she prayed it would. Because she had responsibilities now—big ones—which were eating into her bank account like a swarm of locusts rampaging through a field of maize. She thought about Brittany, her beloved little sister. Brittany, who'd flunked college and become a mother to the adorable Tamsin. Brittany, who was under the dominating rule of Jason, Tamsin's father. Lisa helped out where she could, but she didn't have a bottomless purse and the indisputable fact was that Jason wasn't over-keen on earning money if it involved setting the alarm clock every day. Just as he seemed to have a roving eye whenever any female strayed into his line of vision. But Brittany trusted him, or so she kept saying.

A bitter taste came into Lisa's mouth. Trust. Was there a man alive who could be trusted—and why on earth would any woman ever want to take the risk?

'So pleased you're giving my proposal some serious consideration,' Luc said, his sardonic observation breaking into her thoughts. 'Though I must say that women don't usually take *quite* so long to respond to an invitation to go out with me.'

'I'm sure they don't.'

'Though maybe they would if they realised how much a man enjoys being kept guessing,' he added softly. 'If they knew just how irresistible the unpredictable can be.'

Lisa looked at him. Instinct was telling her to refuse but the voice of common sense was suddenly stronger. It was urging her to stop acting as if millions of offers like this came her way. She thought about the kind of wedding someone like Luc would be attending and all the upmarket guests who would be there. Women with the kind of money who could afford her dresses. Women who wouldn't *dream* of wearing viscose. Surely she'd be crazy to pass up such an opportunity— even if it meant spending the evening with a man who symbolised nothing but danger. She swallowed. And excitement, of course. She mustn't forget that. *But she could resist him. She had resisted him once and she could do it again.*

'Who's getting married?' she questioned carelessly.

He failed to hide his triumphant smile. 'A man named Conall Devlin.'

'The Irish property tycoon?'

'You've heard of him?'

'Hasn't everyone? I read the papers like everyone else.'

'He's marrying a woman named Amber Carter.'

Lisa nodded. Yes. She'd seen pictures of Amber Carter, too—a stunning brunette and the daughter of some industrial magnate. Someone like that would be unbelievably well connected, with friends who might be interested in buying a Lisa Bailey dress. And mightn't this wedding serve another purpose at the same time? Mightn't it get Luc out of her system once and for all if she spent some time with him? Banish some of her dreamy recollections and reinforce some of the other reasons why she'd finished with him. It would do her good to remember his fundamental arrogance and inbuilt need to control. And while she had shared his bed for a while, she realised she didn't really *know* him.

Because Luc hadn't wanted anything deeper— she'd understood that right from the start. He'd made it clear that the personal was taboo and the reason for that was simple. He was a royal prince who could never get close to a foreigner. So there had been no secrets shared. No access to his innermost thoughts just because they'd been sleeping together. He'd said it would be a waste of their time and make their parting all the more difficult if they became more intimate than they needed to be. She had understood and she had agreed, because her own agenda had been the same—if for different reasons—and she had also been determined not to get too close. Not to him. Not to anyone. And so they had just lived in the present—a glorious present which had been all about pleasure and little else.

She returned his questioning look. 'Where is this wedding happening?'

'At Conall's country house at Crewhurst, this Saturday. It's only just over an hour out of London.'

She looked directly into his eyes. 'So it would be possible to get there and back in an evening?'

He held her gaze and she wondered if she'd imagined another flicker of triumph in his smile. 'Of course it would,' he said.

CHAPTER TWO

WHY THE HELL was she *here*? Lisa's fingers tightened around her clutch bag. Alone in a car with the handsome Prince as they approached a stately mansion which was lit up like a Christmas tree.

Had she been crazy to accompany Luc to the A-list wedding of two complete strangers? Especially when she wasn't even sure about his motives for asking her. And meanwhile her own motives were becoming increasingly muddled. She was *supposed* to be concentrating on drumming up new business, yet during a journey which had been short on words but high on tension, all she'd been able to think about was how gorgeous Luc looked in a dark suit which hugged his powerful body and emphasised the deep olive glow of his skin.

The summer sky was not yet dark but already the flaming torches lining the driveway had been lit—sending golden flames sparking into the air and giving the wedding party a carnival feel. On an adjacent field Lisa could see a carousel and nearby a striped hut was dispensing sticks of candyfloss and boxes of popcorn. A smooth lawn lay before them—a darkening sweep of emerald, edged with flowers whose pale colours could still be seen in the fading light.

It looked like a fairy tale, Lisa thought. Like every woman's vision of how the perfect wedding should be. *And you're not going to buy into that.* Because she knew the reality of marriage. She'd witnessed her stepfather crushing her mother's spirit, like a snail being crushed beneath a heavy boot. And even though they weren't even married, she'd seen Brittany being influenced by Jason's smooth banter, which had changed into a steely control once Britt had given birth to Tamsin. Lisa's lips compressed into a determined line. *And that was never going to happen to her. She was never going to be some man's tame pet.*

A valet opened the car door and out she got. One of her high-heeled sandals wobbled as she stepped onto the gravel path, and as Luc put out his hand to steady her Lisa felt an instant rush of desire. Why was it *still* like this? she wondered despairingly as her nipples began to harden beneath her silky dress. Why could no other man ever make her feel a fraction of what she felt for the Prince? She looked into his eyes and caught what looked like a gleam of comprehension and she wondered if he could guess at the thoughts which were racing through her head. Did he realise she was achingly aware of her body through the delicate fabric as she wondered whether he was still turned on by a woman with curves...?

'Look. Here comes the bride,' he said softly.

Lisa turned to see a woman running towards them, the skirt of her white dress brushing against the grass, a garland of fresh flowers on top of her long, dark hair.

'Your Royal Highness!' she exclaimed, dropping a graceful curtsey. 'I'm so happy you were able to make it.'

'I wouldn't have missed it for the world,' answered Luc. 'Amber, do you know Lisa Bailey—the designer? Lisa, this is the brand-new Mrs Devlin.'

'No.' The bride shook her head and smiled. 'I don't believe we've met. I've heard of you, of course—and your dress is gorgeous.'

Lisa smiled back. 'So is yours.'

She was introduced to Amber's new husband Conall—a tall and striking Irishman, who could barely tear his eyes away from his wife.

'We're not having a formal dinner,' Amber was saying, her fingers lacing with those of her groom as they shot each other a look which suggested they couldn't wait to be alone. 'We thought it much better if people could just please themselves. Have fun and mingle. Ride on the carousel, or dance and eat hot dogs. You must let me get you and Lisa a drink, Your Highness.'

But Luc gave a careless wave of his hand. 'No, please. No formality. Not tonight,' he said. 'Tonight I am simply Luc. I shall fetch the drinks myself, which we will enjoy in this beautiful garden of yours, and then I think we might dance.' His eyes glittered as he turned his head. 'Does that idea appeal to you, *chérie*?'

Lisa's heart smashed against her ribcage as his sapphire gaze burnt over her skin and the unexpected French endearment reminded her of things she would prefer to forget. Like the way he used to slide her panties down until she would almost be pleading with him to rip them off—and his arrogant smile just before he did exactly that. But those kinds of thoughts were dangerous. Much. Too. Dangerous.

'I like the sound of looking round the garden,' she said. 'Not having any outside space is one of the drawbacks of living in London, and this is exquisite.'

'Thanks,' said Amber happily. 'And, Luc, you must look out for my brother Rafe, who's over from Australia and prowling around somewhere.

I thought you might like to talk diamonds and gold with him.'

'Of course,' said Luc, removing two glasses of champagne from the tray of a passing waitress and handing one to Lisa. But he barely noticed the newly-weds walk away because all he could focus on was the woman beside him. She looked… He took a mouthful of the fizzy wine, which did nothing to ease the dryness in his throat. She looked *sensational*, in a silvery dress that made her resemble a gleaming fish—the kind which always slipped away, just when you thought you might have captured it. Her shoulders were tense and she was sipping her champagne, determinedly looking everywhere except in his direction.

With a hot rush of hunger he found himself wanting to reacquaint himself with that magnificent body. To press himself up against her. To jerk his hips—hard—and to lose himself inside her as he had done so many times before. He swallowed. Would it be so wrong to sow the last of his wild oats in one glorious finale, before taking up the mantle of duty and marriage which awaited him?

They moved before he had time to answer his own question, making their way across a lawn washed deep crimson by the setting sun where many of the other guests stood talking in small groups. Some of these Luc recognised instantly, for Conall moved in similarly powerful circles.

There were the Irish Ambassador and several politicians, including an Englishman rumoured to be the next-but-one Prime Minister. There was a Russian oil baron and a Greek hotel magnate, and Conall's assistant, Serena, came over with Rafe Carter, the bride's brother—and somehow, in the midst of all the introductions, Lisa slipped away from him.

Yet even though she wasn't next to him, Luc knew exactly where she was as he went through the mechanics of being a dutiful guest. He accepted a bite-sized canapé from a passing waitress and popped it into his mouth, the salty caviar exploding against his tongue. It was an unusual situation— for *him* to be doing the watching, rather than for a woman's eyes to be fixed jealously on him. But she seemed completely oblivious to his presence as she chatted to a clutch of trust-fund babes.

He watched her long curls shimmering down over her tiny frame as she laughed at something one of the women said. He saw a man wander up to the group and say something to her, and Luc's body grew rigid with an unexpected sense of possessiveness.

And suddenly he wanted to be alone with her. He didn't want small talk—or, even worse, to get stuck with someone who was hell-bent on having a serious conversation about his island principality. He didn't want to discuss Mardovia's recent elevation to join the ranks of the world's ten most wealthy islands, or to answer any questions about his new trade agreement with the United States. And he certainly didn't want one of Hollywood's hottest actresses asking quite blatantly whether he wanted her telephone number. Actually, she didn't really put him in a position to refuse—she just fished an embellished little card from her handbag and handed it over, with a husky entreaty that he call her...*soon*. Not wanting to appear rude and intending to dispose of it at the earliest opportunity, Luc slipped the card into his jacket pocket before excusing himself and walking over to where Lisa stood.

There was a ripple of interest as he approached, but he pre-empted the inevitable introductions by injecting an imperious note into his voice. 'Let's go and explore,' he said, taking her half-drunk champagne from her and depositing their glasses on a nearby table. 'I can hear music playing and I want to dance with you.'

Lisa felt a flicker of frustration as he took her drink away, wondering why his suggestions always sounded like *commands*. Because he was a prince, that was why, and he had spent his entire life telling people what to do. Not only was he interrupting her subtle sales pitch, he also wanted to dance with her—an idea which filled her with both excitement and dread. She knew she should refuse, but what could she say? *Sorry, Luc. I'm terrified you're going to hit on me and I'm not sure I'll be able to resist.*

The trouble was that everyone was looking at her and the other women weren't even bothering to hide their envy. Or maybe it was disbelief that such an eligible man wanted to dance with a too-small brunette with an overdeveloped pair of breasts. She wanted to make a break for it, to run towards that copse of trees at the end of the lawn and to lose herself in their darkness. But she hid her insecurity behind the serene mask she'd perfected when her mother had married her stepfather and overnight their world had changed. When she'd learnt never to let people know what you were thinking. It was the first lesson in survival. Act weak and people treated you like a weakling. Act strong and they didn't.

'Okay,' she said carelessly. 'Why not?'

'Not the most enthusiastic response I've ever received,' he murmured as they moved out of earshot. 'Do you get some kind of kick from making me wait?'

Her eyes widened. 'Why? Is it mandatory to answer immediately when spoken to by the Prince?' she mocked.

He smiled. 'Something like that.'

'So why don't you just enjoy the novelty of such an experience?'

'I'm trying.'

'Try harder, Luc.'

He laughed as they walked across the grass to the terrace and up a flight of marble steps leading into the ballroom, from where the sultry sound of jazz filtered out into the warm night air. Lisa's chest was tight as Luc led her onto a quiet section of the dance floor, and as he drew her into his arms she was conscious of the power in his muscular body and the subtle scent of bergamot which clung to his warm skin.

It was hard not to be overwhelmed by his proximity and impossible to prevent the inevitable assault on her senses. This close he was all too real and her body began to stir in response to him. That pins-and-needles feeling spiking over her nipples. That melting tug of heat between her thighs. What chance did she have when he was holding her like this? I haven't danced with a man in a long time, she realised—and the irony was that she'd never actually danced with Luc before. He'd never taken her to a party and held her in his arms like this because their affair had been conducted beneath the radar. And suddenly she could understand why. The hard thrust of his pelvis was achingly evocative as it brushed against her. Dancing was dangerous, she thought. It allowed their bodies to be indecently close in a public place and she guessed that Conall's tight security was the only reason

Luc was okay with that. Anywhere else and people would have been fishing out their cell phones to capture the moment on camera.

Yet somehow, despite her misgivings, she couldn't help but enjoy the dance—at least up to the point where her throat suddenly constricted and her breathing began to grow shallow and unsteady. Had he pulled her closer? Was that why the tips of her breasts were suddenly pushing so insistently against his chest? And if *she* could feel her nipples hardening, maybe so could *he*.

'You seem tense,' he observed.

She moved her shoulders awkwardly. 'Are you surprised?'

'You don't like dancing? Or is being this close to me again unsettling you?'

Lisa drew her head back to meet the indefinable expression in his eyes. 'A little,' she admitted.

'Me, too.'

She pursed her lips together, wishing she could control the thundering of her heart. 'But you must get to dance with hundreds of women.'

'Not at all. I'm not known for my love of dancing.' His finger stroked distractingly at her waist. 'And no woman I've ever danced with makes me feel the way you do.'

'That's a good line, Luc.' She laughed. 'Smooth, yet convincing—and with just the right note of disbelief. I bet you hit the jackpot with it every time.'

'It's not a line.' His brow furrowed. 'And why so cynical?'

'I'd prefer to describe it as having taken a healthy dose of realism and I've always been that way. You never used to object before.'

Reflectively, his finger stroked her bare arm. 'Maybe I was too busy taking off your clothes.'

'Luc—'

'I'm only stating the truth. And please don't give me that breathless little gasp and look at me like that, unless you want me to drag you off to the nearest dark corner.'

'Carry on in that vein and I'll walk off all by myself.'

'Okay.' He sucked in a deep breath before moving his hands to her waist—the slender indentation of her flesh through the delicate silk feeling almost as intimate as if he were touching her bare skin itself. 'Let's keep things formal. Tell me what's been happening in your life.'

'You mean the shop?'

A faint frown arrowed his dark eyebrows together, as if he hadn't meant the shop at all. 'Sure,' he said. 'Tell me about the shop.'

Lisa fixed her gaze on the tiny buttons of his dress shirt. Did she tell him about how empty she'd felt when they'd split, which had made her throw herself headlong into her work—not realising that her ambition was outpacing her and that by aiming so high, she'd made the potential crash back to earth all the harder? 'People kept telling me I ought to expand and so I found myself a backer,' she said. 'Someone who believed in me and was willing to finance a move to a more prestigious part of the city.'

'Who?'

His voice had suddenly roughened and she looked up into his face. 'Is that really relevant?'

'That depends.' There was a pause before he spoke again. 'Is he your lover?'

She screwed up her nose. 'You're implying that I started a relationship with my new backer?'

'Or maybe it was the other way round? Your change in fortune seems a little…dramatic,' he observed. 'It would make sense.'

Her feet slowed on the polished floor and Lisa felt a powerful spear of indignation. Was Luc really coming over as *jealous*—when he'd told her from the get-go that there was never going to be any future in their relationship? Was that what powerful princes did—played at being dog in the manger, not wanting you themselves, but then getting all jealous if they imagined someone else *did*? But she wasn't going to invent a closeness with her backer which did not extend outside the boardroom door. She and Martin were business buddies and nothing more.

She gave a laugh. 'Everyone knows you should

never mix business and pleasure, and I'm afraid there hasn't been time for much in the way of recreation.'

'Why not?'

Again, she moved her shoulders restlessly. 'The stakes are much higher now that I've got the shop and then there's Brittany…'

Her words trailed off but he picked up on her hesitation.

'Your sister?'

Amazed he'd remembered the little sister he'd never even met, Lisa nodded. 'Yes,' she said. 'She had a baby.'

He frowned. 'But she's very young herself, right?'

'Yes, she is and…' Her voice faded because Luc wouldn't be interested in hearing about Brittany's choice of partner. And even though part of her despised Jason and the way he lived, wasn't there still some kind of stubborn loyalty towards him because he was Tamsin's father? 'I've been pretty tied up with that,' she finished.

'So you're an aunt now?' he questioned.

She looked up at him and Luc watched her face dissolve with soppy affection—her green-gold eyes softening and her mouth curving into a wistful smile. He felt a beat of something unfamiliar because he'd never seen her look that way before and a whisper of something he didn't understand crept over his skin.

'Yes, I'm an aunt. I have a little niece called Tamsin and she's beautiful. Just beautiful. So that's my news.' She raised her eyebrows. 'What about you?'

Luc's throat thickened with frustration, because ironically he felt so at ease in her company that Lisa would be the perfect person to confide in. To reveal that soon he would be marrying another woman—the Princess from a neighbouring island who had been earmarked as his bride since birth. A long-anticipated union between two wealthy islands, which he couldn't continue to delay.

And Lisa was a realist, wasn't she? She'd told him that herself. She might even agree that arranged marriages were far more sensible than those founded on the rocky ground of romance, with their notoriously high failure rate. If he hadn't wanted her quite so much he *might* have confided in her, but the truth was that he *did* want her. He wanted her so badly that he could barely move without being acutely aware of his aching groin, and he was glad she was standing in front of him, concealing his erection from any prying eyes.

But something stopped him from starting the inevitable seduction process—something which felt uncomfortably like the fierce stab of his conscience. For a moment he fought it, resenting its intrusion on what should have been a straightforward conclusion to the evening. He knew how much she still wanted him. It was obvious from the way she looked at him—even if he hadn't felt her nipples hardening against his chest or heard the faltering quality of her words, as if she was having difficulty breathing. Just as he knew that his desire for her was greater than anything he'd felt for any other woman. The words he'd spoken while they'd been dancing were true.

But his duty lay elsewhere and he had no right to lose himself in her soft and curvy body. No right to taste her sweetness one last time, because what good would it do—other than trigger a frustration which might take weeks to settle? It wasn't fair to the woman who was intended as his wife, even though it had been twelve months since he'd even seen her. And it wasn't fair to Lisa either.

He remembered that yearning look on her face when she'd spoken about her sister's child—a look which indicated a certain broodiness, as women of her age were programmed to be broody. He needed to let her go to find her own destiny, one which was certainly not linked to his.

Reluctantly, he drew away from her and it was as though he had flicked a switch inside himself.

Self-discipline swamped desire as it had done for the past two years, and, now that sex was off the agenda, he noticed again the pallor of her complexion and faint shadows beneath her eyes. Suddenly, Luc was appalled at his thoughtlessness and ruthlessness. Had he really been planning to satisfy himself with her and then simply walk away and marry another woman?

Yes, he had.

His mouth twisted. *What kind of a man was he?*

'Let's go,' he said abruptly.

'Go?' She looked up at him in bewilderment. 'But it's still early.'

'You're tired,' he said tightly. 'Aren't you?'

She shrugged her shoulders. 'I guess so.'

'And you've probably done all the sales pitching you can for tonight. The party will really get going in a minute and I doubt whether anyone will be asking you how long your turnaround times are or whether you can make them a dress in time for their birthday party. So let's just slip away without a big fuss.'

Aware that she was in no position to object, Lisa nodded but her mood was strangely deflated as they walked towards Luc's waiting car and the sounds of music and laughter grew fainter. For a while back then it had felt so magical and so *familiar* being in his arms again. She'd felt warm and sexy as he'd held her close and his hard body had tensed against hers in silent acknowledgement of the powerful attraction which still pulsed between them. She hadn't thought beyond the dance but had thought they might stay like that for most of the evening. But now, with the moon barely beginning to rise and a trip back to her grotty home in London on the horizon—she felt strangely *cheated*. And embarrassed. As if she had been somehow presumptuous. Because hadn't she wondered if they might end up in bed together? Hadn't that been the one thought which had *really* been on her mind?

Once in the car, she accelerated her Cinderella mood by kicking off the high-heeled shoes and folding herself into one corner of the wide back seat, as if she could simply disappear if she made herself small enough. But Luc didn't react. He simply took out his cell phone and began to read from the screen. It was as if he had retreated from her. As if she were just part of the fixtures and fittings—as inconsequential as the soft leather seat on which they sat.

So don't show him you care, she told herself— even though she could feel the unfamiliar pricking of tears behind her eyes. Had she arrogantly thought he wouldn't be able to keep his hands off her? That he still found her as irresistible as she found him? She closed her eyes and leaned back against the soft leather, wondering if she had misread the whole situation.

Luc stared unseeingly at the screen of his phone until the regular sound of Lisa's breathing told him she was sleeping. It was torture to sit beside her without touching her—when all he wanted to do was to slip his hand beneath her dress and make her wet for him.

He was silent throughout the journey and it was only as they began to edge towards London that he glanced out of the window and began to notice his surroundings. The city was still buzzy as he leaned forward and quietly told the driver to go to Lisa's address.

'You want me to drop you off on the way, boss?' asked the driver.

Luc glanced at his watch. Tempting to call it a night and get away from the enticement she presented, but he owed her more than waking up alone in an empty car. She didn't deserve that. The frown at his brow deepened. She'd never given him any trouble. She hadn't tried to sell her story to the press or to capitalise on her royal connections, had she?

'No,' he said. 'Let's take her home first.'

But he was surprised when the car changed direction and entered the badly lit streets of an unfa-

miliar neighbourhood, where rubbish fluttered on
the pavement and a group of surly-looking youths
stood sucking on cigarettes beneath a lamp post.
Luc frowned as he remembered the ordinary but
very respectable apartment she'd had before. What
the hell was she doing living somewhere like this?

As the car slid to a smooth halt, he reached out
and gently shook her awake.

'Wake up, Lisa,' he said. 'You're home.'

Lisa didn't want to leave the dream—the one
where she was still locked in Luc's arms and he
was about to kiss her. But the voice in her ear
was too insistent to ignore and her eyes fluttered
open to see the Prince leaning over her, his face
shadowed.

Feeling disorientated, she sat up and looked
around. She was home—and she didn't want to
be. Still befuddled, she bent to cram her feet back
into her shoes and picked up her silver clutch bag.
'Thanks,' she said.

'This is where you live?'

She heard the puzzled note in his voice and
understood it instantly. She bet he'd never been
somewhere like this in his privileged life. For a
split second she was tempted to tell him that she
was just staying here while her own home was
being redecorated, but she quickly swallowed the
lie. Why be ashamed of what she was and who
she'd become?

'Yes,' she said, her voice still muzzy from sleep. 'This is where I live.'

'You've moved?' he demanded. 'Why?'

'I told you that Brittany had a baby and the three of them were cramped in a too-small apartment. So…' She shrugged. 'We just did a swap. It made sense. I'm planning to get myself something better when—'

'When business picks up?' he questioned astutely.

'When I get around to it,' she said quickly. Too quickly. 'Anyway, thanks for taking me to the party. Hopefully, I'll have drummed up some new business and it…well, it was good to catch up.'

'Yeah.' Their eyes met. 'I'll see you to the door.'

'Honestly, there's no need.' She flashed him a smile. 'I'm a big girl now, Luc.'

'The subject isn't up for debate,' he said coolly. 'I'll see you to your door.'

The night air was still warm on her bare arms yet Lisa shivered as Luc fell into step beside her. But it wasn't shame about him seeing her home which was bothering her—it was the sudden sense of inevitability which was washing over her. The realisation that this really was goodbye. Fishing the key from her bag, she fumbled with the lock before turning back to face him, unprepared for the painful clench of her heart and an aching sense of loss. She would never see him again, she realised.

Never know that great rush of adrenaline whenever he was close, or the pleasurable ache of her body whenever he touched her. For a split second she found herself wondering why she'd been stupid enough to finish with him, instead of eking out every available second until her royal lover had ended the relationship himself. She'd done it to protect herself from potential heartache, but what price was that protection now?

Sliding her arms around his neck, she reached up on tiptoe and brushed her lips over his. 'Be happy,' she whispered. 'Goodnight, Luc.'

Luc froze as the touch of her lips ignited all his repressed fantasies. He felt it ripple over his skin like the tide lapping over dry sand as he tried to hold back. He told himself that kissing a man was predatory and he didn't like predatory women. He was the master—in charge of every aspect of his life—and he'd already decided that no good could come from a brief sexual encounter.

Yet his throat dried and his groin hardened as the warmth of her body drew him in, because this was different. This was Lisa and her kiss was all the things it shouldn't be. Soft yet evocative—and full of passionate promise. It reminded him of just how hot she'd been in his bed and yet how cool the next morning.

And it was over.

It had to be over.

So why wasn't he disentangling her arms and walking back towards his purring limousine? Why was pushing her through her door and slamming it shut behind them? A low moan of hunger erupted from somewhere deep inside him as he pushed her up against the wall and drove his mouth down on hers.

CHAPTER THREE

LUC WAS AWARE of little other than a fierce sexual need pumping through his veins as he crushed his lips down on Lisa's. He barely noticed the cramped hallway as he levered her up against the peeling wallpaper, or the faint chill of damp in the air as her arms closed around him. He was aware of nothing other than her soft flesh and the hard jerk of the erection which throbbed insistently at his groin.

He kissed her until she cried out his name. Until she circled her hips over his with a familiar restlessness which made him slide his hand underneath the hem of her silver dress. His heart pounded. Her legs were bare and her thighs were cool and he could hear the silent scream of his conscience as his fingertips began their inevitable ascent. He thought about all the reasons why this shouldn't happen, but he was too hot to heed caution and this was too easy. As easy as breathing. He swallowed. With her it always had been that way.

She gave a shuddering little moan as he reached her panties and the sound only fuelled his own hunger.

'Luc,' she gasped.

But he didn't answer. He was too busy sliding the panties aside to provide access for his finger. Too busy reacquainting himself with her moist and eager flesh. He teased her clitoris until she bucked with pleasure and he could smell the earthy scent of sex in the air.

'Hell, you're responsive,' he ground out.

'Are you surprised when you touch me like… *that*?'

Her hands were reaching blindly for his zip and Luc held his breath as she eased it down. His trousers concertinaed to the ground like those of a schoolboy in an alley, and her dextrous hands were now dealing with his boxer shorts—peeling them down until his buttocks were bare. She was cupping his balls and scraping her fingernails gently over their soft swell and in response he reached down and tore her panties apart with a savage rip of the delicate material. Her low laugh reminded him of how much she liked to be dominated in the bedroom and, although his conscience made one last attempt to tell him this was wrong, ruthlessly, he erased it from his mind. Halting her just long enough to remove a condom from his pocket, he tore open the foil with unsteady fingers before sheathing himself.

And then it was happening and there didn't seem to be a damned thing he could do about it. It was as if he were on a speeding train with no idea how to stop. He cupped her bottom so that she could wrap her legs around his hips. Her lips were parted against his cheek and her breasts were flattened against his chest.

'Are you sure you want this?' he whispered, his tip grazing provocatively against her slick flesh.

Her words came out as gasps. 'Are you?'

'I'll give you three guesses,' he murmured and drove deep into her.

His thrusts were urgent and her cries so loud that he had to kiss them silent. It was mindless and passionate and it was over very quickly. She came almost instantly and so did he, hot seed spurting into the rubber and making his body convulse helplessly. He pressed his head against her neck and, as one of her curls attached itself to his lips, he wished it hadn't been so brief. Why the hell hadn't he taken his time? Undressed her slowly and tantalised them both, while demonstrating his legendary control?

He cupped his hand over her pulsating mound, feeling the damp curls tangling in his fingers and enjoying the last few spasms as they died away. Already he could feel himself growing hard and knew from experience that Lisa would like nothing better than to do it all over again. But he couldn't stay for a repeat performance. No way. He needed to get out of there, and fast. To forget this had ever happened and put it to the back of his mind. To get on with his future instead of stupidly allowing himself to be dragged back into the past. He bent down and tugged his trousers back up, struggling to slide the zip over his growing erection, before glancing around the cramped hallway.

'Bedroom?' he questioned succinctly.

She swallowed. 'Third door along.'

It wasn't difficult to find in such a small apartment, and he thought the room was unremarkable except for the rich fabric which covered a sagging armchair and a small vase of fragrant purple flowers on the windowsill. Luc drew the curtains and snapped on a small lamp, intending just to see her safely in bed. To kiss her goodbye and tell her she was lovely—maybe even cover her up with a duvet and suggest she get some sleep. But somehow it didn't quite work out that way. Because once inside her bedroom it seemed a crime not to pull the quicksilver dress over her head and feast his eyes on her body. And an even bigger crime not to enjoy the visual fantasy of her lying on top of the duvet, wearing nothing but an emerald-green bra and a pair of sexy high-heeled shoes.

'Lisa,' he said, thinking how hollow his voice sounded.

In the soft lamplight he could see the bright gleam of her eyes.

She wriggled a little, her thighs parting fractionally in invitation. 'Mmm...?'

Luc knew she was teasing him and that this was even more dangerous. He told himself he didn't want to get back into that special shorthand of lovers or remind himself how good this part of their relationship had always been. Yet somehow his body was refusing to heed the voice of reason as he took her hand and guided her fingers to the rocky hardness at his groin.

'Seems like I want you again,' he drawled.

She laughed as her fingers dipped beneath the waistband and circled his aroused flesh. 'No kidding?'

'What do you think we ought to do about it?' he questioned silkily.

Her voice grew husky as she mimicked his voice. 'I'll give you three guesses.'

His mouth was dry as he undressed them both, impatiently pushing their discarded clothing onto the floor as he reacquainted himself with her curves. He groaned as she caressed the tense muscles of his thighs with those beautiful long fingers. Her curls tickled him as she bent to slide her tongue down over the hollow of his belly. But when she reached the tip of his aching shaft, he grabbed a thick rope of curls.

'No,' he said unsteadily.

'But you like—'

'I like everything you do to me, Lisa, I always did. But this time I want to take it a bit more slowly.' He groaned as he pushed her back against the mattress and leaned over her, his eyes suddenly narrowing. 'But you do realise that this changes nothing? I'm still not in a position to offer you any kind of future.'

Her smile was brittle. 'Don't make this all about you, Luc,' she said. 'It's supposed to be about mutual pleasure.'

A spear of jealousy ran through him. 'And have you had many other lovers?' he questioned. 'A stream of men lying just like this on your bed?"'

'You have no right to ask me something like that.'

'Is that a yes?'

She shook her head but now her voice was shaking with indignation.

'If you must know, there's been nobody since you,' she declared. 'And before you start reading anything into that—don't bother. There hasn't been time for sex, that's all. I've been juggling too many balls and trying to keep my business afloat.' But Lisa knew she wasn't being completely honest as she heard his low laugh of triumph. Of *course* there hadn't been anybody else—because who could compare to the arrogant Prince? Who else could make her feel all the stuff that Luc did? But he didn't want feelings—he wasn't in the market for that and he never had been. Hadn't he just emphasised that very fact? So pretend you don't care. Show him you're independent and liberated and not building stupid fantasies which are never going to happen.

'And just to put your mind at rest, yes—I do realise you're not in the market for a wedding ring,' she added drily.

For a moment she felt him grow tense—as if he was going to say something—and she looked up at him expectantly. But the moment passed and instead he bent his head to kiss her—a kiss that was long and slow and achingly provocative. It made her remember with painful clarity just what she'd been missing. The intimate slide of his fingertips over her skin. The way he could play her body as if he were playing a violin. He grazed his mouth over her swollen breasts, teasing each nipple with his teeth as her hands clutched at the bedclothes beneath her.

She realised she was still wearing her shoes and that the high heels were in danger of ripping through the cotton duvet. She bent one knee to unfasten the buckle but he forestalled her with an emphatic shake of his head.

'No,' he growled as he straddled her, his finger reaching down to caress the leather as if it were an extension of her own skin. 'The shoes stay.'

She could feel the weight of his body and his erection pressing against her belly. He put his hand between her thighs and started to stroke her and Lisa wondered how she could have lived without this for so long.

'Luc,' she breathed as a thousand delicious sensations began to ripple over her.

His thumb stilled. 'You want more?'

She wanted him to hold her tightly and tell her how much he'd missed her, but she was never going to get that. So concentrate on what he can give you.

'Much more,' she said, coiling her arms around his neck. 'I want to feel you inside me again.'

He made her wait, eking out each delicious touch until she was almost weeping with frustration. She could feel the wetness between her thighs as he pushed them apart at last and heard his soft words of French as he entered her.

There was triumph as well as pleasure in his smile as he started to thrust his pelvis and suddenly Lisa wanted to snatch some of the control back. With insistent hands she pushed at his chest and, their bodies still locked, rolled him onto his back so that she was now on top. She saw the light of pleasure which danced in his eyes as she cupped her breasts and began to play with them, tipping her head backwards so that her curls bounced all the way down her back.

'Lisa!' Now it was his turn to gasp as he clamped his hands over her hips, anchoring her to him as their movements became more urgent. He pulled her head down so that he could kiss her, the movement of his tongue mimicking the more intimate thrusts he was making deep inside her.

Lisa shuddered because it felt so real. So *primitive*. This was the most alive she'd felt in a long time. Maybe ever.

She found herself wanting to rake her fingernails over his flesh—even though he'd always been so insistent she shouldn't mark him. But suddenly the desire to do just that was too strong to resist. Caught in a moment made bittersweet by the knowledge that it would never be repeated, she felt the first waves of her orgasm as she touched her lips to his shoulder. The first ripple of pleasure hit her and just before it took her under, she bit him. Bit him and sucked at his flesh like some rookie vampire, and the salty taste of his sweat and his blood on her lips only seemed to intensify her pleasure. His too, judging by the ragged cry he gave as he bucked inside her.

Afterwards she lay there, slumped against his damp body—not wanting to move or speak or to do anything which might destroy the delicious sense of *completeness* which enveloped her.

Go to sleep, she urged him silently as she listened to the muffled pounding of his heart. Go to sleep and let's pretend we're two normal people one last time. I can make you toast and coffee in the morning, and we can sit on stools in my tiny kitchen and forget that you're a prince and I'm a commoner before you walk out of my life for good.

But he was wide awake. She could tell from the tension in his body and the way he suddenly eased himself out of her body. Without a word, he pushed back the sheet and got out of bed.

'Luc?' she questioned, but he had switched on the main light and was walking over to the oval mirror which hung on the wall.

The harsh light emphasised just how cheap the room must look to a man used to palaces—throwing into relief the threadbare rug and the chipped paintwork which she hadn't yet got around to restoring. Tipping his head back, he narrowed his eyes as he studied the bite on his neck, which was already turning a deep magenta colour.

'Bathroom?' he snapped.

'J-just along the corridor,' she stumbled.

He was back some minutes later, having obviously splashed his face with water and raked his fingers through his ruffled black hair in an attempt to tame it. And then her heart clenched with disbelief as he bent down to pick up his clothes and began pulling them on. Surely he wasn't planning on leaving straight away? She'd known it was only ever going to be a one-off but she'd hoped he'd at least sleep with her.

'Is something wrong?' she asked.

'You mean, apart from the fact that you've bitten my neck, like some teenage girl on a first date?' He paused in the act of buttoning up his shirt, his lips tight with anger as he turned to look at her. 'What was the point of that, Lisa? Did you want to make sure you left a trophy mark behind?'

'I know. I know. I shouldn't have done it.' She gave a helpless shrug. 'But you were just too delicious to resist.'

But he didn't smile back. In the glaring light she could see how stony his sapphire eyes looked. He finished dressing and slipped on his shoes. 'I have to go,' he said, giving a quick glance at his watch. 'I shouldn't even be here.'

'Oh?' Her voice was very quiet as she looked at him. 'Have you suddenly decided that my new downmarket accommodation is a little too basic for His Royal Highness? Can't wait to get away now you've had what you came for?'

'Please don't, Lisa,' he said. 'Don't make this any more difficult than it already is. This should never have happened. We both know that.'

She sat up in bed then, her hair falling over her

shoulders as she grabbed at the rumpled sheet to cover her breasts, shielding them from the automatic darkening of his eyes as they jiggled free. 'But you were the one who came into my shop!' she protested furiously. 'The one who practically bribed me into going to that wedding party with you—'

'And you were the one who came onto me on your doorstep when I had already decided to resist you.'

'I didn't hear you objecting at the time!'

'No, you're right. I didn't.' He gave a bitter laugh. 'Maybe I was just too damned weak.'

'Okay. So we were both weak. We wanted each other.' She stared at him. 'But what's the big deal? Why start regretting it now? I mean, it's not as if we're hurting anyone, is it?'

Luc let out a low hiss of air. He didn't want to tell her, but maybe telling her was the only option. The only way she might get the message that this really was the last time and it could never happen again. Yet he wouldn't have been human if he hadn't experienced a sense of regret. His heart clenched in his chest as he looked at her—at the golden-brown curls tumbling down over her milky skin. He stared into the spiky-lashed green-gold of her eyes and felt another unwanted jerk of lust. Another deep desire to go over there and kiss her until there was no breath left in her lungs—until she was parting her thighs and pulling him deep inside her again. And judging from the hunger in her eyes, she was feeling exactly the same.

He wondered if she was aware of just how irresistible he still found her. Perhaps she thought there might be more episodes like this in the future. Maybe she was labouring under the illusion that he would start making regular trips to see her, which would all end up with this seemingly inevitable conclusion. And didn't part of him long for such a delicious scenario?

Yet his sexual hunger was tempered by a deep sense of guilt at what had just happened, because hadn't he just betrayed the woman who had been waiting so patiently for him on the island of Isolaverde? Hadn't he broken his self-imposed celibacy— big time—and with the very last woman he should have chosen?

'I'm afraid it is a big deal,' he said slowly.

She looked at him and grew completely still, as if sensing from the sudden harshening of his voice that she was about to hear something she would prefer not to.

'I don't understand.'

'There's someone else.'

The words hung in the air between them and for a moment they were met with nothing other than a disbelieving silence before her shoulders stiffened in shock.

'Someone else?' she repeated blankly.

'Yes.'

'You mean…?' she managed at last, her green-gold eyes icing over. 'You mean you're sleeping with two women at the same time? Or is that a little conservative of me? Maybe there are more than two—are you operating some sort of out-dated harem?'

'Of course I'm not!' he gritted back. 'And it isn't that simple. Or that easy.'

'Oh, Luc. Your tortured face is a picture. You poor thing! My heart bleeds for you.'

'I have been betrothed to a princess since she was a child,' he said heavily.

'Betrothed?' Lisa gave a brittle little laugh, as if sarcasm could protect her from the pain which was lancing through her heart. As if it would blind her to the fact that she had misjudged him. Worse, she had trusted him. She hadn't asked him for the stars but she had expected him to behave with some sort of integrity towards her. *But why should she expect integrity when she knew how ruthless men could be?* 'This is the twenty-first century, Luc. We don't use words like *betrothed* any more.'

'Where I come from, we do. It's the way things work in my country.' He picked up one of his gold cufflinks which were lying next to the vase of purple flowers. 'The way they've always worked, ever since—'

'Please! I don't want a damned lesson in Mardovian history!' she hissed. 'I want you to tell me how you've just had sex with me if there's…someone else.'

He clipped first one cufflink and then the other, before lifting his eyes to hers. 'I'm sorry.'

'You *bastard*.'

'I made it very clear from the beginning that there could never be any future between us. I always knew that my destiny was to marry Sophie.'

Sophie. Somehow knowing her name made it even worse and Lisa started to tremble.

'But you didn't think to tell me that at the time.'

'At the time there was no reason to tell you, for she and I had an agreement that we should both lead independent lives until the time of the wedding approached.'

'And now it has.'

'Now it has,' he agreed, and his voice was almost gentle. Like a doctor trying to find the kindliest way of delivering a deadly diagnosis. 'This was my last foreign trip before setting the matrimonial plans in motion.'

'And you thought you'd have one final fling— with the woman who would probably ask the least questions?'

'It wasn't like that!' he said hotly.

'No? What, you just *happened* to come into my shop last week?'

'I wanted to tie off some of the loose ends in my life.'

There was a pause. Lisa had never imagined herself being described as a *loose end* and something told herself to kick him out. To get his cheating face out of her line of vision and then start trying to forget him. But she didn't. Some masochistic instinct made her go right ahead and ask the question. 'What's she like? *Sophie.*'

He winced, as if she had committed some sort of crime by saying the Princess's name out loud while she sat amid sheets still redolent with the scent of sex.

'You don't want to know,' he said roughly.

'Oh, but that's where you're wrong, Luc. I do. Indulge me that, at least. I'm curious.'

There was a brief pause before he answered. 'She is young,' he said. 'Younger even than you. And she is a princess.'

Lisa closed her eyes as suddenly she wished this night had never happened. Because if he hadn't come back she would never have known about Sophie. Luc would have existed in her imagination as the perfect lover she'd had the strength to walk away from and not as the duplicitous cheat he really was. 'And how does she feel, knowing just what her precious fiancé is up to the moment her back is turned?' she questioned in a shaking voice. 'Or doesn't she mind sharing you with another woman?'

'I have never been intimate with Sophie!' he bit out. 'Since tradition dictates she will come to me as a virgin on our wedding night.' He paused as he surveyed her from between his lashes, his expression suddenly sombre. 'Because that is my destiny and the duty which has been laid down for me since the moment of my birth. And a prince must always put duty, Lisa, above all else. That has always been my guiding principle.'

She shook her head, terrified she was going to do something stupid, like picking up the vase of purple flowers and hurling it at him. Or bursting into useless tears. 'You wouldn't know the meaning of the word *principle* if it was staring out of a dictionary at you!'

His voice tensed, but he forged on—sounding as if someone had written him a script and he was reading from it. 'And once my ring is on her finger, I will stray no more.'

Lisa closed her eyes. So that was all she was to him. Someone to 'stray' with. Like a stray cat— lost and hungry and taken in by the first person to offer it a decent meal. What a stupid mistake she'd made. She'd let herself down. She'd tarnished the past and muddied the present. And all because of one little kiss. Because she'd reached up and brushed her lips over his and the whole damned thing had got out of hand.

So show some dignity. Don't scream and rage.

Don't let his last memory of you be of some woman on the rampage because he's passing you over for someone else. Because she had never given him access to her emotions and she wasn't about to start now. Bitterness and vitriol were luxuries she couldn't afford, because she might not have much—but she still had her pride. She opened her eyes and met the sapphire glint of his, only now she barely noticed their soft blaze—just as she no longer saw the beauty in his olive-skinned features. All she saw was duplicity and deceit.

'Just go, Luc,' she said.

He hesitated and for a moment she thought he might be about to come over to the bed and kiss her goodbye, and she tried to tell herself that she would slap his cheating face if he attempted *that*—because how was it possible to want something and to fear it, all at the same time? But he didn't. He just turned and walked out of the bedroom and Lisa slumped back on the pillows and lay there, listening to the sounds of his leaving. The front door clicked shut and she heard the thud of his footsteps on the pavement before a door slammed and his powerful car pulled away.

She lay there until she needed to go to the bathroom and then padded across the room to where her discarded green panties lay and beside them a small, cream-coloured card, which must have fallen from his trouser pocket.

She picked it up and stared at it and a feeling of self-disgust rippled over her shivering skin. She'd thought it wasn't possible to feel any worse than she already did but she was wrong. Oh, Luc, she thought. How *could* you? He had taken her to a party and had sex with her afterwards—but had still managed to bag himself a calling card from the beautiful Hollywood actress she'd seen at the wedding.

Compressing her lips together to stop them from trembling, Lisa crushed the card between her fingers and dropped it into the bin.

CHAPTER FOUR

'JASON THINKS YOU'RE PREGNANT.'

Lisa almost dropped the toddler-sized dress she had been in the process of folding and slowly turned her head to stare at her sister. They were sitting side by side on the carpet as they sorted out Tamsin's clothes, deciding which ones would still fit her for the cold winter months ahead. But now the tiny dress dangled forgotten from her fingers as she looked into green-gold eyes so like her own. 'What…did you say?'

Brittany appeared to be choosing her words with care. 'Jason says you've got the same look I had when I was carrying Tamsin. And I've noticed that you've stopped wearing your own dresses, which struck me as kind of strange.' Brittany gave a little wriggle of her shoulders. 'Since you've always told me that wearing your own dresses was your best advertisement. And you've never been the kind of woman to slop around in jeans and a loose shirt before.'

Lisa didn't answer as she put the dress down and picked up a tiny pair of dungarees, knowing she was playing for time but not caring. She didn't owe Brittany an explanation. Or Jason, for that matter. Especially not Jason—who was so fond of judging other people but who never seemed to take the time to look at his own grasping behaviour.

But Jason's scrounging was irrelevant right now, because somehow he had unwittingly hit on the truth and passed it on to her sister—and the hard fact remained that she *was* starting to show. At just over sixteen weeks Lisa guessed that was inevitable. Unless she was still in that horrified state of denial which had settled over her at the beginning, when the countless pregnancy tests she'd taken had all yielded the same terrifying results—but at least they'd explained why she'd felt so peculiar. Why her breasts had started aching in a way which was really uncomfortable. Eventually, she had taken herself off to the doctor, who had pronounced her fit and healthy and then smilingly congratulated her on first-time motherhood. And if Lisa's response had been fabricated rather than genuine, surely that wasn't surprising. Because how could she feel happy about carrying the child of a man who no longer wanted her? A man who was about to marry another woman?

'So who's the father?' questioned Brittany.

'Nobody you know,' said Lisa quickly.

There was a pause. 'Not that bloke you used to go out with?'

Lisa stiffened. 'Which bloke?'

'The one you were so cagey about. The one you never wanted anyone to meet.' Brittany sniffed. 'Almost as if you felt we weren't good enough for him.'

Lisa bit her lip. It was true she'd never introduced Brittany or Jason to the Prince—and not just that she had been worried that Jason might attempt to 'borrow' money from the wealthy royal without any intention of ever paying it back. She'd known there was no future in the relationship and therefore no point of merging their two very different lives.

And she didn't want to bring Luc into the conversation now. If she told her sister that she was expecting the child of a wealthy prince, Brittany would inevitably tell Jason and she wouldn't put it past him to go hawking the story to the highest bidder. 'I'd rather not discuss the father,' she said.

'Right.' Brittany paused. 'So what are you going to do?'

'Do?' Lisa sat back on her heels and looked at her sister blankly. 'What do you mean, *do*?'

'About the *baby*, of course! Does he know?'

No, he didn't know—though she'd done her best to try to contact him. Lisa chewed on her lip. Even that had been another stark lesson in humiliation.

She had tried to ring him on the precious number she still had stored in her phone—but the number was no longer in service. Of course it wasn't. So she'd summoned up all her courage to telephone the palace in Mardovia, somehow managing to get through to one of his aides—a formidable-sounding woman called Eleonora. But Eleonora had stonewalled all her attempts to speak to the Prince and, short of blurting out her momentous news on the phone, Lisa had eventually given up—because how could she possibly disclose something like that to a member of Luc's staff?

And if she was being totally honest, she had been slightly relieved, thinking perhaps it was better this way. He was due to marry another woman. Someone called Princess Sophie—a woman who had never done *her* any harm. How could she ruin her life by announcing that an impulsive one-night stand had resulted in another woman carrying his baby? Damn Luc Leonidas, Lisa thought viciously. Damn him for not bothering to tell her about his impending marriage *before* he'd jumped into bed with her.

'No,' Lisa said, steeling herself against the curiosity in her sister's eyes. 'He doesn't know and he isn't going to. He doesn't want to see me again and he certainly doesn't want to be a father to my child. So I'm going to bring this baby up on my own and it's going to be a happy and well-cared-for baby.'

'But, Lisa—'

'No, please. Don't.' Lisa shook her head, feeling little beads of sweat at the back of her neck and so she scooped up the great curtain of curls and waved it around to let the air refresh her skin. She looked pointedly at her sister, her gaze intended to remind her of the harsh truth known to both of them. That a child brought up in a home with a resentful man was not a happy home. 'I'm not asking your opinion on this, Brittany,' she said quietly. 'I'm just telling you how it's going to be.'

There was a pause. 'Is he married?'

Not yet.

'No comment. Like I said, the discussion is over.' Lisa gave a grimace of a smile as she rose to her feet. 'But you've given me an idea.'

'*I* have?' Brittany looked momentarily puzzled.

'Yes. I keep saying that you're much cleverer than you give yourself credit for.' Lisa narrowed her eyes, her mind suddenly going into overdrive. 'And if I'm going to spend the next few months getting even bigger, I might as well do it in style.'

Brittany's green-gold eyes narrowed. 'What's that supposed to mean?'

'It means that although I've had a few extra orders since I went to that fancy wedding back in August, it hasn't been enough to take the business forward as I'd hoped. What I need is a completely new direction—and I think I've just found one.'

Lisa sucked in a deep breath as she patted her expanding stomach. 'Think about it. There aren't many really fashionable maternity dresses on the market right now—especially ones in natural fabrics, which "breathe". I can work in more fabrics than just my trademark silk. Cotton and linen and wool. There's an opportunity here staring me right in the face, and it seems I'm the perfect person to model my new collection.'

'But…won't that get publicity?'

Lisa smiled and it felt like the first genuine smile she'd given in a long time. 'I sincerely hope so.'

'You aren't afraid that the father will hear about it and come to find you?'

Lisa shook her head. No. That was one thing she *wasn't* worried about. Luc certainly wouldn't be trawling the pages of fashion magazines now that he'd turned his back on his playboy life and locked himself away on his Mediterranean principality. Luc had made his position very clear.

'No,' she said quietly. 'He won't find out.'

She sat back on her heels and as a rush of something like hope flooded through her, so did a new resolve. She needed to be strong for her baby and that wasn't going to happen if she sat around wailing at the unfairness of it all. She was young, fit and hard-working and she had more than enough love to give this innocent new life which was growing inside her.

Her baby *would* be happy and well cared for, she vowed fiercely. No matter what it took.

Luc sat at his desk feeling as if he had just opened Pandora's box. The blood pounded inside his head and his skin grew clammy. There must be some kind of mistake. There *must* be. He had been bored. Why else would he have tapped Lisa's name into the search engine of his computer? Yet wasn't the truth something a little more unpalatable? That he couldn't get her out of his head, no matter how hard he tried.

Nearly six months had passed since he'd seen her and he had been eaten up with guilt about what had happened just before he'd left London. He had broken his self-imposed celibacy with his ex-lover, instead of the woman he was due to marry. But he was over that now and the date for his wedding to Sophie was due to be announced next week. It was the end of an era and the beginning of a new one, and he intended to embrace it wholeheartedly. And that was why he had typed Lisa's name into the search engine—as a kind of careless test to see whether he could now look on her with indifference.

A muscle at his temple flickered as once again

he stared with disbelief at the screen. He was no stranger to shock. He had lost his mother in the most shocking of circumstances—and in some ways he had lost his father at the same time. He had thought nothing would ever rock him like that again, but a faint echo of that disbelief reverberated through him now. He stared at the image in front of him and his mouth dried. A picture of Lisa at a fashion show. Her lustrous caramel curls were pulled away from her face and her eyes and skin seemed to glow with a new vitality—but it hadn't been that which had made his blood run cold.

He stared at her swollen belly. At the hand which lay across her curving shape in that gently protective way which pregnant women always seemed to adopt. Features hardening into a frown, he read the accompanying text.

DESIGNER LAUNCHES SWELL NEW LINE!
Lisa Bailey, famous for the understated dresses which captivated a generation of 'Ladies Who Lunch', last night launched her new range of maternity wear. And stunning Lisa just happened to be modelling one of her own designs!

Coyly refusing to name the baby's father, the six-months-pregnant St Martin's graduate would say only that, 'Women have successfully been bringing up children on their own for centuries. It's hardly ground-breaking stuff.'

Ms Bailey's collection is available to buy from her Belgravia shop.

Luc sat back in his chair.

Lisa, *pregnant*? He felt the ice move from his veins to his heart. It couldn't be his. Definitely not his. He shook his head as if his denial would make it true, but memories had started to crowd into his mind which would not be silenced. Her heated claim that there had been no other lover than him since they'd been apart—and he had *believed* her, because he knew Lisa well enough to realise she wouldn't lie about something like that. Six months pregnant. He sat back in his chair, his heart pounding as he raked a strand of hair away from his heated face. Of *course* it was his.

Lisa Bailey was carrying his baby.

His baby.

Disbelief gave way to anger as he shut down the computer. Why the hell hadn't she told him? Why had she left him to find out in such a way—and, just as importantly, who else knew?

He reached out for the phone, but withdrew his hand again. He needed to think carefully and not act on impulse, for this was as delicate a negotiation as any he had ever handled. Using the phone would be unsatisfactory and there was no guar-

antee the call wouldn't be overheard by someone at her end. Or his. It occurred to him that she
might refuse to speak to him—in fact, the more
he thought about it, the more likely a scenario that
seemed, for she could be as stubborn as hell.

Leaning forward, he pressed the buzzer on his
desk and Eleonora appeared almost immediately.

'Come in and close the door.' Luc paused for a
moment before he spoke. 'I want you to cancel everything in my diary for the next few days.'

Her darkly beautiful face remained impassive.
'That might present some difficulties, Your Royal
Highness.'

Luc regarded her sternly. 'And? Is that not
what I pay you for—to handle the tricky stuff and
smooth over any difficulties?'

'Indeed.' Eleonora inclined her dark head. 'And
does Your Royal Highness wish me to make any
alternative arrangements to fill the unexpected
spaces in your diary?'

Luc's mouth flattened as he nodded. 'I need to
fly to Isolaverde and afterwards I want the plane
on standby, ready to take me to London.'

'And am I allowed to ask why, Your Royal
Highness?'

'Not yet, you're not.'

Eleonora bit her lip but said nothing more and
Luc waited until she had left the office before
slowly turning to stare out of the window at the

palace gardens. Already the days hinted at the warm weather ahead, yet his heart felt as wintry as if it had been covered with layers of ice. He couldn't bear to sit here and think about the unthinkable. He wanted to go to England now. To go to Lisa Bailey and…and…

And what? His default mechanism had always been one of action, but it was vital he did nothing impulsive. He must think this through carefully and consider every possibility which lay open to him.

The following morning he flew to Isolaverde for the meeting he was dreading and from there his jet took him straight to London—but by the time he was sitting in his limousine outside Lisa's shop, his feelings of disbelief and anger had turned into a clear focus of determination.

The evening was cold and a persistent drizzle had left the pavements shining wet, with a sickly orange hue which glowed down from the streetlights. In the window of Lisa's shop was a pregnant mannequin wearing a silk dress, her hand on her belly and a prettily arranged heap of wooden toys at her feet. Luc had sat and watched a procession of well-heeled women being dropped off by car or by taxi, sheltered from the rain by their chauffeurs' umbrellas as they walked into the shop. Business must be booming, he thought grimly.

He forced himself to wait until the shop closed

and a couple of women who were clearly staff had left the building. As Luc waited, a passing police officer tapped on the window of the limousine, discreetly overlooking the fact that it was parked on double yellow lines once he was made aware of the owner's identity.

He waited until the lights in the shop had been dimmed and he could see only the gleaming curls of the woman sitting behind a small desk—and then he walked across the street and opened the door to the sound of a tinkly bell.

Lisa glanced up as the bell rang, wondering if a customer had left their phone behind or changed their mind about an order—but it was nothing as simple as that. It felt like a case of history repeating itself as Luc walked into her shop, only this time there wasn't a look of curiosity on his face which failed to conceal the spark of hunger in his eyes. This time she saw nothing but fury in their sapphire depths—though when she stopped to think about it, could she really blame him?

Yet she had stupidly convinced herself that this scenario would never happen—as if some unknown guardian angel were protecting her from the wrath of the man who stood in front of her, his features dark with rage. She was glad to be sitting down, because she thought her knees might have buckled from the shock of seeing him standing there—trying to control his ragged breathing.

He didn't have to say a word for her to know why he was here; it was as obvious as the swell of her belly, which he was staring at like a man who had just seen a ghost.

Don't be rash, she reasoned, telling herself this was much too important to indulge her own feelings. She had to think about the baby and only the baby.

'Luc,' she said. 'I wasn't expecting you.'

He lifted his gaze from her stomach to her face as their eyes met in a silent clash. 'Weren't you?' he said grimly. 'What's the matter, Lisa? Surely you must have known I would turn up sooner or later?'

She licked her suddenly dry lips. 'I tried not to think about it.'

'You tried not to think about it?' he repeated. 'Is that why I was left to discover via social media that you're pregnant?'

'I didn't mean—'

'I don't care what you did or didn't mean because you're going to have a baby.' Ruthlessly, he cut across her words. But for the first and only time since she'd known him, he seemed to be struggling with the rest of the sentence, because when finally he spoke, he sounded choked. '*My* baby.'

Lisa could feel the blood draining from her face and thought how wrong this all seemed. A miracle of life which should—and did—fill her with joy and yet the air around them throbbed with accusation and tension. Her hands were unsteady and she felt almost dizzy, and all she could think was that this kind of emotion couldn't be good for the baby. 'Yes,' she breathed at last, staring down at the tight curve of her belly as if to remind herself. 'Yes, I'm having your baby.'

There was an ominous silence before he spoke again. A moment when he followed the direction of her gaze, staring again at her new shape as if he couldn't believe it.

'Yet you didn't tell me,' he accused. 'You kept it secret. As if it was your news alone and nobody else's. As if I had no right to know.'

'I did try to tell you!' she protested. 'I tried phoning you but your number had changed.'

'I change my number every six months,' he informed her coldly. 'It's a security thing.'

Lisa pushed a handful of hair away from her hot face. 'And then I phoned the palace and got through to one of your aides. Eleonora, I think her name was.'

Luc's head jerked back. 'You spoke to Eleonora?'

'Yes. And she told me that you weren't available. Actually, it went further than that. She said I wasn't on your list of telephone contacts. If you must know she made me feel like some pestering little groupie who needed to be kept away from the precious Prince at all costs.'

Luc let out a long sigh. Of course she had. Eleonora was one of his most fiercely loyal subjects, and part of her role had always been to act as his gatekeeper, and never more so than when he'd returned to Mardovia following his illicit night with Lisa. When he'd been full of remorse for what he'd done but unable to shake off the erotic memories which had clung to his skin like the soft touch of her fingers. He had thrown himself into his work, undertaking a punishing schedule which had taken him to every town and city on the island. And he had instructed his fiercely loyal aide not to bother him unless absolutely necessary.

'You could have written,' he said.

'What, sent you a postcard, or a letter which was bound to be opened by a member of your staff? Saying what? *Dear Prince Luciano, I'm having your baby*?' Her gaze was very steady. 'You told me you were going to marry another woman. You made it very clear you never wished to see me again. And after you'd gone, I found a card on my bedroom floor—a card from some Hollywood actress you must have met at the wedding. My lowly place in the pecking order was confirmed there and then.'

'I could tell you that I took the card simply as a politeness with no intention of contacting her again, but that is irrelevant,' he gritted out. 'Because the bottom line is that you're pregnant, and we're going to have to deal with that.'

She shook her head. 'But there's nothing to deal with. You don't have to worry. I have no wish to upset your fiancée or your plans for the future. And lots of women have children without the support of men!' she finished brightly.

'So you said in your recent interview,' he agreed witheringly.

'And it doesn't matter what you say.' She looked at him defiantly, because defiance made her feel strong. It stopped her from crumpling to the ground and just opening her mouth and *howling*. It stopped her from wishing he would cradle her in his arms, like any normal father-to-be—his face full of wonder and tenderness. She licked her lips. 'Because when it boils down to it, this is just a baby like any other.'

'But that's where you're wrong, Lisa,' he negated softly. 'It *is* different. This is not *just a baby*. The child you carry has royal blood running through its veins. Royal Mardovian blood. Do you have any idea of the significance of that?' His face hardened. 'Unless that was the calculated risk you took all along?'

She stared at him in confusion. 'I'm not sure I understand.'

'No?' The words began to bubble up inside him, demanding to be spoken and, although years of professional diplomacy urged Luc to use caution, the shock of this unexpected discovery was making him want to throw that caution to the wind. 'Maybe this is what you hoped for all along,' he accused. 'I saw your face at the wedding when you started talking about your niece. That dreamy look which suggested you longed to become a mother yourself. I believe women often become broody when they're around other people's children. When their body clock is ticking away as yours so obviously is. Is that what happened to you, Lisa? Only instead of saddling yourself with a troublesome partner as your sister seems to have done—maybe you decided to go it alone.'

'You're *insane*,' she breathed. 'Completely insane.'

'Am I? Don't they say that children are the new accessories for the modern career woman? Was that why you threw yourself at me that night, when I was trying to do the honourable thing of resisting you?' He gave a bitter laugh. 'Was that why you made love to me so energetically—riding me like some rodeo rider on a bucking bronco? Perhaps hoping to test the strength of the condom we used—because you wanted my seed inside you. It is not unknown.'

She stared at him in disbelief as his words flooded over her in a bitter stream. 'Or maybe I went even further?' she declared. 'Perhaps you

think I was so desperate to have your child that I
went into the bathroom after you'd gone and per-
formed some sort of amateur DIY insemination?
That's not beyond the realms of possibility either!'

'Don't be so disgusting!' he snapped.

'Me?' She stared at him. 'That's rich. You're the
one who came in here making all kinds of bizarre
suggestions when all I wanted was to try to do
the decent thing—for everyone concerned. You're
going to marry Sophie and...' She stood up then,
needing to move around, needing to bring back
some blood to her cramped limbs. Leaving behind
the clutter of her desk, she walked over to a rail of
the new maternity dresses which she'd worked so
hard on—pretty dresses which discreetly factored
in the extra material needed at the front. She'd
been feeling so proud of her new collection. She'd
taken lots of new orders after the show and had
allowed herself the tentative hope that she could
carry on supporting Brittany and Tamsin and still
make a good life for herself and her own baby. Yet
now, in the face of Luc's angry remarks—her will
was beginning to waver.

She straightened a shimmery turquoise dress
before forcing herself to meet his gaze. 'Don't you
understand that I'm letting you off the hook? I
don't want to mess up your plans by lumbering
you with a baby you never intended to have. A
commoner's baby. You're going to be married to

someone else. A princess.' The hurt she'd managed
so successfully to hide started to creep up, but she
forced herself to push it away. To ask the question
she needed to ask and to try to do it without her
voice trembling, which suddenly seemed like one
of the hardest things she'd ever had to do. 'Because how the hell do you think Princess Sophie
is going to feel when you tell her you're going to
be a father?'

CHAPTER FIVE

'SHE KNOWS,' SAID LUC, the words leaving his mouth as if they were poison. 'Princess Sophie knows about the baby and it's over between us.'

He watched Lisa grow still, like an animal walking through the darkened undergrowth suddenly scenting danger. Her green-gold eyes narrowed as she looked at him and her voice was an uncertain tremble.

'B-but you said—'

'I know what I said,' he agreed. 'But that was then. This is now. Or did you really think I was going to take another woman as my wife when you are pregnant with my child? This changes everything, Lisa.' There was a heartbeat of a pause. 'Which is why I went to see the Princess before I came to England.'

She winced, closing her eyes briefly—as if she was experiencing her own, private pain. 'And what…what did she say?'

Luc picked his words carefully, still trying to

come to terms with the capriciousness of women. He didn't understand them and sometimes he thought he never would. And when he stopped to think about it—why should he, when the only role models he'd known had all been paid for out of the palace purse?

He had been expecting a show of hurt and contempt from his young fiancée. He had steeled himself against her expected insults as he had been summoned into the glorious throne room of her palace on Isolaverde, where shortly afterwards she had appeared—an elegant figure in a gown of palest blue which had floated around her. But the vitriol he deserved hadn't been forthcoming.

'She told me she was relieved.'

'*Relieved?*'

'She said that a wedding planned when the bride-to-be was still in infancy was completely outdated and my news had allowed her to look at her life with renewed clarity. She told me that she didn't actually *want* to get married—and certainly not to a man she didn't really know, for the sake of our nations.' He didn't mention the way she had turned on him and told him that she didn't approve of his reputation. That the things she'd heard and read in the past—exploits which some of his ex-lovers had managed to slip to the press—had appalled her. She had looked at him very proudly and announced that maybe fate was doing her a favour by freeing her from her commitment to such a man. And what could he do but agree with her, when he was in no position to deny her accusations? 'So I am now a free man,' he finished heavily.

Lisa's response to this was total silence. He watched her walk over to the desk and pour herself a glass of water and drink it down very quickly before turning back to face him. 'How very convenient for you,' she said.

'And for you, of course.'

Abruptly, she put the glass down. 'Me?' The wariness in her green-gold eyes had been replaced by a glint of anger. 'I'm sorry—you've lost me. What does the breaking off of your engagement have to do with me? We had a one-night stand with unwanted consequences, that's all. Two people who planned never to see one another again. Nothing has changed.'

Luc studied her defensive posture, knowing there were better methods of conveying what he needed to say and certainly more suitable environments in which to do so than the shop in which she worked. But he didn't have the luxury of time on his side—for all kinds of reasons. His people would be delighted by news that his royal bloodline would be continued, but he doubted they'd be overjoyed to hear that the royal mother was an unknown commoner and not their beloved Princess Sophie. He would have to ask the Princess to issue a dignified announcement before introducing Lisa as his bride, for that would surely lessen the impact. And he would get his office to start working on image control—on how best to minimise the potential for negative repercussions for him and for Mardovia.

'Everything has changed,' he said. 'For I am now free to marry you.'

Lisa's heart missed a beat, but even in the midst of her shock she reflected what cruel tricks life could play. Because once Luc's words would have affected her very differently. When she'd been starting to care for him…really care. When she'd been standing on the edge of that terrifying precipice called love. Just before she'd pulled back and walked away from him—she would have given everything she possessed to hear Luc ask her to marry him.

And now?

Now she accepted that the words were as empty as a politician's sound bites. The mists had cleared and she saw him for who he really was. A powerful man who shifted women around in his life like pawns in a game of chess. Why, even his brides were interchangeable! Princess Sophie had been heading for the altar, only to be cast aside with barely a second thought because a pregnant commoner counted for more than a virgin princess.

And now *she* was expected to step in and take her place as his bride. Poor Sophie. And poor *her*, if she didn't grow a backbone.

She drew in a deep breath. 'You really think I'd *marry* you, Luc?'

The arrogant smile which curved his mouth made it clear he thought her protest a token one.

'I agree it isn't the most conventional of unions,' he said. 'But given the circumstances, you'd be crazy not to.'

Lisa could feel herself growing angry. Almost as angry as when she'd looked down at her dead mother's face and thought how wasted her life had been. She remembered walking away from the funeral parlour hoping that she had found peace at last.

She'd been angry too when Brittany had dropped out of her hard-fought-for place at one of England's top universities because Jason had wanted her to have his baby, and nothing Lisa had said could talk her sister out of it, or make her wait. Another woman who had allowed herself to be manipulated by a man.

But maybe she no longer had a right to play judge and jury when now she found herself in a situation which was wrong from just about every angle. She stared into Luc's face but saw no affection on his rugged features—nothing but a grim determination to have things on *his* terms, the way he always did. And she couldn't afford to let him—because if she gave him the slightest leeway, he would swamp her with the sheer force of his royal power.

'I think we'll have to disagree on the level of my craziness,' she said quietly. 'Because you must realise I can't possibly marry you, Luc, no matter what you say—or how many inducements you make.'

His sudden stillness indicated that her reply had surprised him.

'I don't really think you have a choice, Lisa,' he said.

'Oh, but that's where you're wrong. There is always a choice. And mine was to have this child alone and to love it with all my heart. It still is.'

'But I am the father.'

'I know you are. And now that it's all out in the open you must realise that I shan't deny you access to your child.' She smiled up at him. 'We'll keep emotion out of it and try to come to some satisfactory arrangement for all of us.'

He didn't smile back.

'You seem to forget that you carry a prince or princess,' he said softly. 'And it is vital they should grow up on the island they will one day inherit.'

She met his gaze. 'I didn't realise illegitimate offspring were entitled to inherit.'

A muscle began to flicker at Luc's temple because this conversation wasn't going according to plan. His marriage proposal had been intended to pacify her and possibly to thrill her. To have her eating out of his hand—because women had been trying to push him towards the altar most of his adult life and deep down he had imagined Lisa would be no different. He'd thought she would be picturing herself walking down the wide aisle of Mardovia's famous cathedral—a glittering tiara in her curly hair. Yet all she was doing was surveying him with a proud look and he felt the slow burn of indignation. Who the *hell* did she think she was—turning down his offer of marriage without even a moment's consideration?

For a split second he felt powerless—an unwelcome sensation to someone whose power had always been his lifeblood. He wanted to tell her that she *would* do exactly as he demanded and she might as well resign herself to that fact right now. But the belligerent expression on her face told him he had better proceed with caution.

His gaze drifted over her, but for once the riot of curls and green-gold eyes were not the focus of his attention. He noted how much fuller her breasts were and how the swell of her belly completely dwarfed her tiny frame. *And inside that belly was his child.* His throat thickened.

She looked like a tiny boat in full sail, yet she was no less enticing for all that. He still wanted her and if circumstances had been different he might have pulled her in his arms and started to kiss her. He could have lulled her into compliance and taken her into one of those changing rooms. Drawn the velvet curtains away from prying eyes and had her gasping her approval to whatever it was he asked of her.

But she was heavy with child. Glowing like a pomegranate in the thin winter sun—and because of that he couldn't use sex as a bargaining tool.

'Get your coat,' he said. 'And I'll take you home.'

'I haven't finished what I was doing.'

'I'll wait.'

'There's no need. Honestly, I can get a cab.'

'I said, I'll wait. Don't fight me on this, Lisa—because I'm not going anywhere.' And with this he positioned himself on one of the velvet and gilt chairs, stretching his long legs in front of him.

Lisa wanted to protest, but what was the point? She couldn't deny they needed to talk, but not now and not like this—when she was still flustered by his sudden appearance and the announcement that he'd called off his wedding. She needed to have her wits about her but her brain currently felt as if it were clouded in mist, leaving her unable to think properly. And that was dangerous.

He had taken out his cell phone and was flicking through his emails and giving them his full attention, and she found herself almost envying him.

If only she were capable of such detachment of thought! The figures in front of her were a jumble and in the end she gave up trying to make sense of them. How could she possibly concentrate on her work with Luc distracting her like this?

She shut down her computer and gave him a cool look. 'Okay. I'm ready,' she said.

She sensed he was exerting considerable restraint to remain patient as she carried the jug and water glass out into the kitchen, set the burglar alarm, turned off the lights and locked the door. Outside, the drizzle was coming down a little heavier now and his driver leapt from the car to run over and position a huge umbrella over her head. She wanted to push the monstrous black thing away—uncaring that the soft rain would turn her hair into a mass of frizz—but she stopped just in time. She needed to be calm and *reasonable* because she suspected that she and Luc were coming at this pregnancy from completely different angles. And if she allowed her fluctuating hormones to make her all volatile, he would probably get some awful Mardovian judge to pronounce her unfit to be a mother!

She sat in frozen silence on the way to her apartment and a feeling of frustration built up inside her when he made no attempt to talk to her. Was he playing mind games? Trying to see which of them would buckle first? Well, he had better realise that this wasn't a game—not for her. She was strong and resolute and knew exactly what she wanted.

But when they drew up outside her humble block, he surprised her with his words.

'Have dinner with me tomorrow night.'

'Dinner?'

'Why not?' he said. 'We need to discuss what we're going to do and there's nothing in the rule-book which says we can't do it in a civilised manner.'

In the dim light Lisa blinked. She thought about the two of them making an entrance in the kind of fancy restaurant he would no doubt frequent— the handsome Prince and the heavily pregnant woman.

'But if we're seen out together,' she said slowly, 'that would be making a fairly unequivocal statement, wouldn't it? A prince would never appear alone in public with a woman in my condition unless he was willing to be compromised. Is that what you want, Luc?'

His eyes glittered as he leaned towards her. 'Yes,' he said. 'That's exactly what I want. I *want* the world to know that I am the father. You have my child in your belly, Lisa. Do you really think I intend to relinquish my claim on my own flesh and blood?'

The words sounded almost *primitive* and they

were filled with a sense of possession. They reminded Lisa of the full force of his power and the fact that he had grown up with very different values from her. 'Of course I don't!' she said. 'We can meet with a lawyer and have a legal agreement drawn up. You can see your child any time you like—within reason. Surely you can have no objection to that?'

His eyes were cold and so was his voice. 'I think you are missing the point, *chérie*. I intend to marry you.'

'I'm sorry, Luc.' She gave a slight shake of her head as she reached for the door handle. 'I'm afraid that's just not going to happen.'

But he leaned across the seat and placed his hand over her forearm, and Lisa hated the instant ripple of recognition which whispered over her skin the moment he touched her. Did he feel it, too—was that why he slid his thumb down to her wrist as if to count the beats of the rocketing pulse beneath?

'Let me see you to your door,' he said.

The set of his jaw told her that objection would be a waste of time and so she shrugged. 'Suit yourself. But you're not coming in.'

Luc made no comment as he accompanied her to her front door as he'd done what now seemed a lifetime ago. But this time there was no warmth and light gilding the summer evening into a golden blur which matched their shared desire. This time there was only the cold bite of a rainy night and a barely restrained sense of hostility. But she was pregnant, he reminded himself. *Inside her beat the tiny heart of his own flesh and blood. And that changed everything.*

Luc was not a sentimental man and emotion had been schooled out of him from an early age, but now he became aware of something much bigger than himself. He stared at her swollen frame with the realisation that here lay something more precious than all the riches in his entire principality. And he was shaken by just how badly he wanted it.

'I don't want to have to fight you to get what I want, Lisa,' he said softly as they reached her door. 'But if you force my hand then I'm afraid that's what's going to happen. Perhaps I should warn you now that it is better not to defy me.'

Her eyes narrowed like those of a cornered cat. 'If only you could hear yourself!' she retorted, unlocking her front door and pushing it open. 'I can defy you all I like! I'm a free spirit—not your possession or your subject. This is the twenty-first century, Luc, and you can't make me do something I don't want to—so why don't we resume this discussion in the cold light of day when you're ready to see sense?'

His powerful body grew still and for one hopeful moment Lisa thought he was about to take her advice. But she was wrong. He lifted his hand to rake his fingers back through his rain-spangled hair and she hated the sudden erotic recall which that simple gesture provoked.

'Your backer is a man called Martin Lawrence,' he said slowly.

She didn't ask how he knew. She didn't show her surprise or foreboding as she raised her eyebrows. 'And?'

'And yesterday afternoon he sold all his interest in your business to me.'

It took her a few seconds to process this and once the significance hit her, she shook her head. 'I don't believe you,' she said. 'Martin wouldn't do that. He wouldn't. Not without telling me.'

'I'm afraid he did.' A cynical smile tugged at the corners of his mouth. 'The lure of money is usually enough to eclipse even the most worthy of principles and I offered him a price he couldn't refuse.'

'You…bastard,' she said, walking like a robot into her hallway, too dazed to object when he followed her and snapped on the harsh overhead light. But this time there were no frantic kisses. No barely controlled hunger as they tore at each other's clothes. There was nothing but a simmering mistrust as Lisa stared into his unyielding blue eyes. 'So what are you planning to do?' she questioned. 'Dramatically cut my funds? Or slowly bleed me dry so that you can force me into closure?'

'I'm hoping it won't come to that,' he said. 'My acquisition of your business was simply a back-up. An insurance policy, if you like, in case you proved to be stubborn as I anticipated, which is exactly what has happened. But I have no desire to be ruthless unless you make me, Lisa. I won't interfere with your business if you return to Mardovia with me as my wife.'

She shook her head. 'I can't do that, Luc,' she breathed. 'You know I can't.'

'Why not?' His gazed bored into her. 'Is it because I'm the wrong man? Are you holding out for Mr Right? Is that what this is all about?'

She gave a short laugh. 'Mr Right is a fictional character created by women who still believe in fairy tales. And I don't.'

'Well, isn't that just perfect, because neither do I. Which means that neither of us have any illusions which can be shattered.'

But his declaration gave Lisa little comfort. Her back was aching and her feet felt swollen. She walked into the tiny sitting room and slumped into one of the overstuffed armchairs without even bothering to put the light on. But Luc took control of this, too, following her and snapping on a lamp before drawing the curtains against the darkness outside. She found herself thinking that his servants must usually do this kind of thing for him and wondered what it must be like, to live his privileged life.

'We don't have to go through with a sham marriage,' she said wearily. 'I told you. We can do this the modern way and share custody. Lots of people do. And given all the wealth at your disposal, it will be easier for us to achieve than for most people.' From somewhere she conjured up a hopeful smile. 'I mean, it's not like we're going to be worried about whether we can afford to run two households, is it?'

But he didn't respond to her feeble attempt at humour.

'You're missing the point,' he said. 'I have a duty to my people and the land I was born to rule. Mardovia's stability has been threatened in the past and the principality was almost destroyed as a result. It cannot be allowed to happen again and I will not let it. This child is the future of my country—'

'What? Even if it's a girl?'

He went very still. 'Do you *know* the sex of the baby?' he questioned.

Lisa thought about lying. Of saying she was going to have a girl in the hope that the macho rules which seemed to define him would make him reconsider his demand that she marry him. But she couldn't do that. It would be a cheap move to use their baby as a pawn in their battle, and she sensed it wouldn't make any difference.

She shook her head. 'No. I told the sonographer I didn't want to know. I didn't like the idea of going through a long labour without even the promise of a surprise at the end. A bit like getting your Christmas presents and discovering that nobody had bothered to wrap them.'

He smiled at this and, inexplicably, Lisa felt herself softening. As if nature had programmed her to melt whenever the father of her child dished out some scrap of affection. *And she couldn't afford to melt.*

'Whatever the sex of the baby, there's no reason why the act of succession cannot be re-examined some time in the future,' he said and walked across the room towards her, towering over her, his muscular body completely dominating her line of vision. 'I am doing my very best to be reasonable here and I will do everything in my power to accommodate your desires, Lisa. And before you start glowering at me like that, I wasn't referring just to physical desires, though I'm more than happy to take those into account.'

Lisa could feel her face growing hot and her breasts beginning to prickle. And the most infuriating thing of all was that right then she wanted him to touch them again. To cup and fondle them and flicker his tongue over them. She wanted him to put his hand between her legs and to ease the aching there. Was it *normal* for a pregnant woman to feel such a powerful sense of desire?

'I can't do that,' she said in a low voice. 'My life is here. I can't leave my little niece, or my sister.'

'Why not?'

'Because I…help them.'

'What do you mean, you help them?'

She shrugged. 'They have no regular income.'

'Your sister is a single parent?'

'Sort of. She's with Jason, only they're not married and he's rather work-shy.'

'Then it's about time he changed his attitude,' he said. 'Your sister and child will receive all the support they require because I will be able to help with that, too. And soon you will have a family of your own to think about.'

'And my business?' she demanded, levering herself into a sitting-up position and trying to summon the energy to glare at him. 'What about that? I've worked for years to establish myself and yet now I'm expected to drop everything—as if my work was nothing but some disposable little hobby.'

'I am willing to compromise on that and I don't intend to deprive you of your career,' he said softly. 'You have people who work for you. Let them run the shop in your absence while you design from the palace.'

And Lisa knew that whatever objection she raised Luc would override her. Because he could. He didn't care that she was close to her little niece and terrified that everything she'd worked for would simply slip away if she wasn't there to oversee it. He didn't care about her—he never had. All he cared about was what *he* wanted. And he wanted this baby.

'You don't understand.' She raised her hands in a gesture of appeal, but the answering look in his eyes was stony.

'I understand more than you might think,' he said. 'I shall accommodate your wishes as much as possible. I don't intend to be a cruel husband. But be very clear about one thing, Lisa—that this topic is not open for debate. That if it comes to it, I will drag you screaming and kicking to the altar, because you *will* be my wife and my child *will* be born on Mardovian soil.'

There was a pause as she bit her lip before looking up at the grim determination which made his blue eyes look so cold. 'If…if I agree to this forced marriage, I want some form of compensation.'

'Compensation?' he echoed incredulously, as if she was insulting him—which in a way she guessed she was. Unless you counted what she wanted as some old-fashioned kind of dowry.

'Yes,' she said quietly. 'I want you to buy my sister a house of her own and provide her with a regular income which will free her from the clutches of her sponging partner.'

His mouth twisted. 'And that is the price for your consent?'

Lisa nodded. 'That is my price,' she said heavily.

CHAPTER SIX

Luc looked around the room—a relatively small room but the one where his wedding to Lisa Tiffany Bailey was about to take place. It was decked out with garlands of flowers, their heavy fragrance perfuming the air, and over the marble fireplace was the crimson and gold of the Mardovian flag. Everything around him was as exquisitely presented as you would expect in the embassy of a country which had a reputation for excellence—and the staff had pulled out all the stops for the unexpected wedding of their ruler to his English bride. But when it boiled down to it, it was just a room.

His face tightening with tension, he thought about the many generations of his family who had married in the august surroundings of the famous cathedral in Mardovia's capital. Grand weddings attended by other royals, by world leaders, politicians and aristocracy. Huge, glittering affairs which had been months in the planning and talked about for years afterwards.

But there would be no such wedding for him.

Because how could he marry in front of his traditionally conservative people with such a visibly pregnant bride in tow? Wouldn't it flaunt his own questionable behaviour, as well as risking offending Princess Sophie—a woman adored by his subjects? This was to be a small and discreet ceremony, with a woman who did not want to take part in it.

He allowed himself a quick glance at the chairs on which her small family sat. The sister who looked so like her, and her boyfriend Jason, who Lisa clearly didn't trust. *Just as she didn't trust him.* Luc watched the casually dressed man with the slightly too long hair glance around the ornate room, unable to hide his covetous expression as he eyed up the lavish fixtures and fittings. He sensed Lisa was disappointed that the new house and income which had been given to her sister had failed to remove Jason from the equation. It seemed that her sister's love for him ran deep...

But her dysfunctional family wasn't the reason he was here today and Luc tensed as the Mardovian national anthem began to play. Slowly, he turned his head to watch as Lisa made her entrance, his heart pounding as she started to walk towards him and he was unprepared—and surprised—by the powerful surge of feeling which ran through him as she approached.

His mouth dried to dust as he stared at his bride, thinking how *beautiful* she looked, and he felt the inexplicable twist of his heart. More beautiful than he could ever have imagined.

She had left her hair spilling free—a glossy cascade broken only by the addition of white flowers which had been carefully woven into the honeyed locks. To some extent, the glorious spectacle of her curls drew the eye away from her rounded stomach, but her dressmaker's eye for detail had also played a part in that—for her gown was cleverly designed to minimise the appearance of her pregnancy. Heavy cream satin fell to her knee and the matching shoes showcased shapely legs which, again, distracted attention from her full figure. And, of course, the gleaming tiara of diamonds and pearls worn by all Mardovian brides drew and dazzled the eye. Beside her, with one chubby little hand clinging on tightly, walked the toddling shape of her little niece—her only bridesmaid.

And then Luc looked into Lisa's face. At the unsmiling lips and shuttered eyes, and a sense of disappointment whispered over him. She certainly wasn't feigning a joy she clearly didn't feel! Her expression was more suited to someone about to attend their own execution rather than their wedding.

Yet could he blame her? She had never sought closeness—other than the purely physical variety. This must be the last thing in the world she wanted. His jaw tightened. And what about him? He had never intended for this to happen either. Yet it *had* happened. Fate had presented him with a very different kind of destiny from the one mapped out for him, and there wasn't a damned thing he could do about it. He stared at her as a powerful sense of certainty washed over him. Except vow to be the best father and husband he could possibly be.

Could he do that?

'Are you okay?' he questioned as she reached his side.

Okay? Chewing on her lip, Lisa bent to direct her little niece over to the ornate golden chair to sit beside her mother. No, she was *not* okay. She felt like a puppet. Like a *thing*. She was being dragged into matrimony like some medieval bride who had just been bought by her powerful master.

But if she was being forced to go through with this marriage, maybe she ought to do it with at least the *appearance* of acceptance. Wouldn't it be better not to feed the prejudices of his staff when she sensed they already resented his commoner bride? So she forced a smile as she stepped up beside Luc's towering figure.

'Ecstatic,' she murmured and met the answering glint in his eyes.

The ceremony passed in a blur and afterwards

"FAST FIVE" READER SURVEY

Your participation entitles you to:
✳ 4 Thank-You Gifts Worth Over $20!

Complete the survey in minutes.

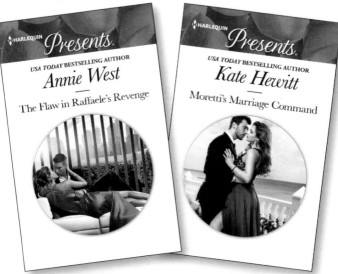

Get **2 FREE** Books

Your Thank-You Gifts include **2 FREE BOOKS** and **2 MYSTERY GIFTS**. There's no obligation to purchase anything!

See inside for details.

Dear Reader,

Since you are a lover of our books, your opinions are important to us... and so is your time.

That's why we made sure your **"FAST FIVE" READER SURVEY** can be completed in just a few minutes. Your answers to the five questions will help us remain at the forefront of women's fiction.

And, as a thank-you for participating, we'd like to send you **4 FREE THANK-YOU GIFTS!**

Enjoy your gifts with our appreciation,

Pam Powers

To get your
4 FREE THANK-YOU GIFTS:

✱ Quickly complete the "Fast Five" Reader Survey
and return the insert.

▶ DETACH AND MAIL CARD TODAY!

"FAST FIVE" READER SURVEY

1	Do you sometimes read a book a second or third time?	○ Yes ○ No
2	Do you often choose reading over other forms of entertainment such as television?	○ Yes ○ No
3	When you were a child, did someone regularly read aloud to you?	○ Yes ○ No
4	Do you sometimes take a book with you when you travel outside the home?	○ Yes ○ No
5	In addition to books, do you regularly read newspapers and magazines?	○ Yes ○ No

YES! I have completed the above Reader Survey. Please send me my 4 FREE GIFTS (gifts worth over $20 retail). I understand that I am under no obligation to buy anything, as explained on the back of this card.

❏ I prefer the regular-print edition
106 HDL GJ5D/306 HDL GJ5D

❏ I prefer the larger-print edition
176 HDL GJ5D/376 HDL GJ5D

FIRST NAME   LAST NAME

ADDRESS

APT.#   CITY

STATE/PROV.   ZIP/POSTAL CODE

Offer limited to one per household and not applicable to series that subscriber is currently receiving.
Your Privacy—The Reader Service is committed to protecting your privacy. Our Privacy Policy is available online at www.ReaderService.com or upon request from the Reader Service. We make a portion of our mailing list available to reputable third parties that offer products we believe may interest you. If you prefer that we not exchange your name with third parties, or if you wish to clarify or modify your communication preferences, please visit us at www.ReaderService.com/consumerschoice or write to us at Reader Service Preference Service, P.O. Box 9062, Buffalo, NY 14240-9062. Include your complete name and address.

© 2016 HARLEQUIN ENTERPRISES LIMITED
® and ™ are trademarks owned and used by the trademark owner and/or its licensee. Printed in the U.S.A.

P-816-SFF15

READER SERVICE—Here's how it works:

Accepting your 2 free Harlequin Presents® books and 2 free gifts (gifts valued at approximately $10.00) places you under no obligation to buy anything. You may keep the books and gifts and return the shipping statement marked "cancel." If you do not cancel, about a month later we'll send you 6 additional books and bill you just $4.30 each for the regular-print edition or $5.30 each for the larger-print edition in the U.S. or $5.24 each for the regular-print edition or $5.74 each for the larger-print edition in Canada. That is a savings of at least 12% off the cover price. It's quite a bargain! Shipping and handling is just 50¢ per book in the U.S. and 75¢ per book in Canada.* You may cancel at any time, but if you choose to continue, every month we'll send you 6 more books, which you may either purchase at the discount price or return to us and cancel your subscription. *Terms and prices subject to change without notice. Prices do not include applicable taxes. Sales tax applicable in N.Y. Canadian residents will be charged applicable taxes. Offer not valid in Quebec. Books received may not be as shown. All orders subject to approval. Credit or debit balances in a customer's account(s) may be offset by any other outstanding balance owed by or to the customer. Please allow 4 to 6 weeks for delivery. Offer available while quantities last.

▲ If offer card is missing write to: Reader Service, P.O. Box 1867, Buffalo, NY 14240-1867 or visit www.ReaderService.com ▲

BUSINESS REPLY MAIL
FIRST-CLASS MAIL   PERMIT NO. 717   BUFFALO, NY

POSTAGE WILL BE PAID BY ADDRESSEE

READER SERVICE
PO BOX 1867
BUFFALO NY 14240-9952

NO POSTAGE
NECESSARY
IF MAILED
IN THE
UNITED STATES

there was a small reception. But an overexcited Tamsin started running around and ground some wedding cake into an antique rug, and Lisa didn't like the way Jason seemed to be hovering over a collection of precious golden artefacts sitting on top of a beautiful inlaid table.

It was Luc who smoothly but firmly brought the proceedings to an end—and Lisa had to swallow down the sudden tears which sprang to her eyes as she hugged her little niece goodbye, before clinging tightly to her sister.

'I'm going to miss you, Britt,' she said fiercely.

And Brittany's voice wobbled as she hugged her back. 'But you'll be back, won't you, Lisa? My lovely new house is certainly big enough to accommodate my princess sister,' she whispered. 'Or we can come out and stay with you in Mardovia. We'll still see each other, won't we?'

Lisa met her sister's eyes. How did you tell your closest relative you were terrified of being swallowed up by an alien new life which would shut out the old one for good? With a deep breath, she composed herself. You didn't. You just got on with things and made the best of them, the way she'd done all her life. 'Of course we will,' she said.

'Are you ready, Lisa?' came Luc's voice from behind her and she nodded, glad that confetti was banned on the surrounding fancy London streets—because she honestly didn't think she could smile like some happy hypocrite as she walked through a floating cloud of rose petals.

A car whisked them to the airfield, where they were surrounded by officials. Someone from the Aviation Authority insisted on presenting Lisa with a bouquet, which only added to her feelings of confusion because she wasn't used to people curtseying to her. It wasn't until they were high in the sky over France that she found herself alone with Luc at last, and instantly she was subjected to a very different kind of confusion—a sensual tug-of-war which had become apparent the moment the aircraft doors had closed and they were alone together.

He had changed from his Mardovian naval uniform and was wearing a dark suit which hugged his powerful frame, and his olive skin looked golden and glowing. His long legs were spread out in front of him and, distractingly, she couldn't stop remembering their muscular power and the way he had shuddered with pleasure as she had coiled her fingertips around them. Her mouth dried and she wondered if he knew how uncomfortable she was feeling as his sapphire gaze rested thoughtfully on her.

'Now, as weddings go…' he elevated his black brows in a laconic question '…was that really so bad?'

She shrugged. 'That depends what you're comparing it with. Better than being adrift at sea for three days with no water, I suppose—though probably on a par with being locked up for life and having the key thrown away.'

'Oh, Lisa.' The brief glint of amusement which had entered his eyes was suddenly replaced with a distinct sense of purpose. 'Your independent attitude is something I've always enjoyed but this marriage isn't going to work if you're going to spend the whole time being obstructive.'

'And what did you think I was going to do?' she questioned, her voice low because she was aware that although the officials were out of sight, they were still very much present. 'Fall ecstatically into your arms the moment you slid the ring on my finger?'

'Why not? You wouldn't hear any objection from me and it's pretty obvious that the attraction between us is as powerful as it ever was—something which was demonstrated on the night our baby was conceived. And now we're man and wife,' he said, sliding his hand over her thigh and leaving it to rest there, 'isn't that what's supposed to happen? Isn't it a pity to let all this frustrated desire go to waste?'

Lisa stared down at the fingers which were outlined against the grey silk jersey of her 'going away' dress and thought how right they felt. As if they had every right to be there—ready to creep beneath the hem of her dress. Ready to slip inside her panties, which were already growing damp with excitement. She thought about the pleasure he was capable of giving her. Instant pleasure which could be hers any time she liked.

But something told her that she shouldn't slip into intimacy with him—no matter how tempting the prospect—because to do so would be to lose sight of his essential ruthlessness. He had brought her here like some kind of *possession*. An old-fashioned chattel who carried his child. He had married her despite all her protestations, and there hadn't been a thing she could do about it. She was trapped. The deal had been sealed. She had made her bed and now she must lie in it.

She just didn't intend sharing it with him.

That was the only thing she was certain of—that she wasn't going to complicate things by having sex with a man who had blackmailed her to the altar. Her resistance would be the key to her freedom, because a man with Luc's legendary libido would never endure a sexless marriage. Inevitably, he would be driven into the arms of other women and she would be able to divorce him on grounds of infidelity. She pushed his hand away, telling herself it was better this way. Better never to start something which could only end in heartache. But that didn't stop her body from missing that brief caress of his fingers, from wishing that she could close her eyes and pretend not to care when they slipped beneath her dress and began to pleasure her…

'We may be married,' she said. 'But it's going to be in name only.'

'Do I take that to mean you're imposing a sex ban?' he questioned gravely.

She smoothed down the ruffled silk jersey, which still bore the imprint of his hand, and waited until her heart had stopped racing quite so much. 'A ban would imply that something was ongoing, which is definitely not the case. We had one night together—and not even a whole night because you couldn't wait to get away from me, could you, Luc? So please don't try suggesting that I'm withdrawing something which never really got off the ground.'

Luc frowned, unused to having his advances rejected, or for a woman to look at him with such determination in her eyes. His power and status had always worked in his favour—but it was his natural *charisma* which had always guaranteed him a hundred per cent success rate with the opposite sex. Yet he could sense that this time was different. Because *Lisa* was different. She always had been. He remembered the silent vow he had taken as she'd walked towards him in all her wedding finery. A vow to be the best husband he could. She was a newly crowned princess and she was *pregnant*—so shouldn't he cut her a little slack?

'I hear what you say,' he said. 'But the past is

done, Lisa. All we have is the present. And the future, of course.'

'And I need you to hear this,' she answered, in a low and fervent voice. 'Which is that I will perform my role as your princess, at least until after the birth. But I will be your wife in name only. I meant what I said and I will not share a bed with you, Luc. I don't intend to have sex with you. Be very clear about that.'

'And is there any particular reason why?' His eyes mocked her, his gaze lingering with a certain insolence on the swell of her breasts. 'Because you want me, Lisa. You want me very badly. We both know that.'

There was silence for a moment as Lisa willed her nipples to stop tingling in response to his lazy scrutiny. She swallowed. 'Because sex can weaken women. It can blind them to the truth, so that they end up making stupid mistakes.'

'And you have experience of this, do you?'

She shrugged. 'Indirectly.'

His voice was cool. 'Are you going to tell me about it? We need something to do if we aren't going to celebrate our union in the more conventional manner.'

Lisa hesitated. As usual, his words sounded more like an order than a question and her instinct was to keep things bottled up inside her, just as she'd always done. He'd never been interested in this kind of thing in the past, but she guessed things were different now. And maybe Luc needed to know why she meant what she said. To realise that the stuff she'd experienced went bone deep and she wasn't about to change. She didn't *dare* change. She needed to stay exactly as she was—in control. So that nobody could get near to her and nobody could ever hurt her. 'Oh, it's a knock-on effect from my scarred childhood,' she said flippantly.

Pillowing his hands behind his dark head, he leaned back in the aircraft seat and studied her. 'What happened in your childhood?'

It took a tense few moments before the words came out and that was when she realised she'd never talked about it before. Not even with Britt. She'd buried it all away. She'd shut it all out and put that mask on. But suddenly she was tired of wearing a mask all the time—and she certainly had no need to impress Luc. Why, if she gave him a glimpse into her dysfunctional background, maybe he might do them both a favour and finish the marriage before it really started.

'My father died when my sister and I were little,' she said. 'I was too young to remember much about him and Britt was just a baby. He was much older than my mother and he was rich. Very rich.' She met his sapphire gaze and said it before he could. 'I think that was the reason she married him.'

'Some women crave security,' he observed with a shrug.

She had expected condemnation, not understanding, and slowly she let out the breath she hadn't even realised she'd been holding. 'She was brought up in poverty,' she said slowly. 'Not the being-broke-before-payday kind, but the genuine never knowing where your next meal is coming from. She once told me that if you'd ever experienced hunger—*real* hunger—then you never forgot it. And marrying my father ensured that hunger became a thing of the past. When he died she became a very wealthy woman...'

'And?' he prompted as her voice trailed off, his eyes blue and luminous.

'And...' Lisa hesitated. She had tried to understand her mother's behaviour and some of it she could. But not all. She compressed her lips to stop them wobbling. 'She found herself in the grip of lust for the first time in her life and decided to reverse her earlier trend by marrying a man much younger than herself. A toy boy,' she finished defiantly. 'Although I don't believe the word was even invented then.'

'A man more interested in her money than in a widow with two young children to care for?'

She gazed at him suspiciously. 'How did you know that?'

'Something in your tone told me that might be

the case, but I am a pragmatist, not a romantic, Lisa,' he said drily. 'And all relationships usually involve some sort of barter.'

'Like ours, you mean?' she said.

'I think you know the answer to that question,' he answered lightly.

She stared down at the silk-covered bump of her belly before lifting her gaze to his again. 'He wasn't a good choice of partner. My stepfather was an extremely good-looking man who didn't know the meaning of the word fidelity. He used to screw around with girls his own age—and every time he was unfaithful, it broke my mother just a little bit more.'

'And that affected you?'

'Of course it affected me!' she hit back. 'It affected me *and* my sister. There was always so much *tension* in the house! One never-ending drama. I used to get home from school and my mother would just be sitting there gazing out of the window, her face all red and blotchy from crying. I used to tidy up and cook tea for me and Britt, but all Mum cared about was whether or not *he* would come home that night. Only by then he'd also discovered the lure of gambling and the fact that she was weak enough to bankroll it for him, so it doesn't take much imagination to work out what happened next.'

His dark lashes shuttered his eyes. 'He worked his way through her money?'

Lisa stared at him, trying not to be affected by the understanding gleam in his eyes and the way they were burning into her. But she *was* affected.

'Lisa? What happened? Did he leave you broke?'

She thought she could detect compassion in his voice, but she didn't want it. Because what if she grew to like it and started relying on it? She might start wanting all those things which women longed for. Things like love and fidelity. Things which eluded them and ended up breaking their hearts. She forced herself to remember Luc's own behaviour. The way he'd coldly left her in bed on the night their child had been conceived. The way he'd focussed only on the mark she'd left on his neck instead of the fact that he had *used* her. And that there was some poor princess waiting patiently in her palace for him to return to marry her. Kind Princess Sophie who had been generous enough to send them a wedding gift, despite everything which had happened.

So don't let on that it was a stark lesson in how a man could ruin the life of the women around him. Let him think it was all about the money. He would understand that because he was a rich man and rich men were arrogant about their wealth. Lisa swallowed. He'd shown no scruples about buying out her business and exerting such powerful control over her life, had he? So tell him what he expects

to hear. Make him think you're a heartless bitch
who only cares about the money.

'Yeah,' she said flippantly. 'The ballet lessons
had to stop and so did the winter holidays. I tell
you, it was hell.'

She saw the answering tightening of his lips
and knew her remark had hit home. And even
though she told herself she didn't *care* about his
good opinion, it hurt to see the sudden distaste on
his face. Quickly, she turned her head towards the
window and looked out at the bright blue sea as
they began their descent into Mardovia.

CHAPTER SEVEN

'AND THIS,' SAID LUC, 'is Eleonora.'

Lisa nodded, trying to take it all in. The beautiful green island. The white and golden palace. The child kicking frantically beneath her heart. And now this beautiful woman who was staring at her with an expression of disbelief—as if she couldn't quite believe who Luc had married.

'Eleonora has been my aide for a number of years,' Luc continued. 'But I have now assigned her to look after you. Anything you want or need to know—just ask Eleonora. She's the expert. She knows pretty much everything about Mardovia.'

Lisa tried to portray a calm she was far from feeling as she extended her hand in greeting. She felt alone and displaced. She was tired after the flight and her face felt sticky. She wanted to turn to her new husband and howl out her fears in a messy display of emotion which was not her usual style. She wanted to feel his strong arms wrapped protectively around her back, which would be the biggest mistake of all. So instead she just fixed a smile to her lips as she returned Eleonora's cool gaze.

She wondered if she was imagining the unfriendly glint in the eyes of the beautiful aide. Did Eleonora realise that Lisa had been feeling completely out of her depth from the moment she'd arrived on the island and her attitude wasn't helping? The aide was so terrifying elegant—with not a sleek black hair out of place and looking a picture of sophistication in a slim-fitting cream dress, which made Lisa feel like a barrel in comparison. Was she looking at her and wondering how such a pale-faced intruder had managed to become Princess of Mardovia? She glanced down at her bulky tum. It was pretty obvious how.

Lisa sucked in a deep breath. Maybe she was just being paranoid. After all, she couldn't keep blaming Eleonora for not putting her in touch with Luc that time she'd telephoned. She hadn't known Lisa was newly pregnant because Lisa hadn't told her, had she? She'd only been doing her job, which was presumably to protect the Prince from disgruntled ex-lovers like her.

So she smiled as widely as she could. 'It's lovely to meet you, Eleonora,' she said.

'Likewise, Your Royal Highness,' said Eleonora, her coral lips curving.

Luc glanced from one woman to the other.

'Then I shall leave you both to become better acquainted.' He turned towards Lisa. 'I have a lot of catching up to do so I'll see you at dinner. But for now I will leave you in Eleonora's capable hands.'

Lisa nodded, because what could she say? *Please don't go. Stay with me and protect me from this woman with the unsmiling eyes.* She and Luc didn't have that kind of relationship, she reminded herself, and she was supposed to be an independent woman. So why this sudden paralysing fear which was making her feel positively *clingy*? Was it the see-sawing of her wretched hormones playing up again?

In silence Lisa watched him go, the sunlight glinting off his raven hair and the powerful set of his shoulders emphasising his proud bearing. Suddenly the room felt empty without him and the reality of her situation finally hit home. She was no longer ordinary Lisa Bailey, with a failing shop, a mortgage and a little sister who was being dominated by a feckless man. She was now a princess, married to a prince adored by all his people—and all the curtseying and bowing was something she was going to have to get used to.

And despite all her misgivings, she couldn't help but be entranced by the sun-drenched island. During the drive to Luc's palace, she had seen rainbows of wild flowers growing along the banks of the roads and beautiful trees she hadn't recognised. They had passed through unspoiled villages where old men sat on benches and watched the world go by in scenes which had seemed as old as time itself. Yet as they had rounded a curve in one of the mountain roads she had looked down into a sparkling bay, where state-of-the-art white yachts had dazzled like toys in an oversized bathtub. It had been at that point that Lisa had realised that she was now wife to one of the most eligible men in the world.

'You would like me to show you around the palace?' questioned Eleonora in her faultless English.

Lisa nodded. What she would have liked most would have been for Luc to give her a guided tour around his palatial home, but maybe that was asking too much. She could hardly tell him she had no intention of behaving like a *real* wife and then expect him to play the role of devoted husband. And mightn't it be a good idea to make an ally out of his devoted aide? To show a bit of genuine sisterhood? She smiled. 'I should like that very much.'

'You will find it confusing at first,' said Eleonora, her patent court shoes clipping loudly on the marble floors as they set off down a long corridor. 'People are always taken aback by the dimensions of the royal household.'

'Were you?' questioned Lisa as she peeped into a formal banqueting room where a vast table was adorned with golden plates and glittering crystal goblets. 'A bit shell-shocked when you first came here?'

'Me?' Eleonora's pace slowed and that coral-lipped smile appeared again. 'Oh, no. Not at all. My father was an aide to Luc's father and I grew up in one of the staff apartments on the other side of the complex. Why, the palace is the only home I've ever really known! I know every single nook and cranny of the place.'

Lisa absorbed this piece of information in silence, wondering if she was supposed to feel intimidated by it. But she wasn't going to *let* herself be intimidated. She had been upfront with Luc and maybe she should be just as upfront with his aide—and confront the enormous elephant which was currently dominating the palatial corridor.

'I know that Luc was supposed to marry Princess Sophie,' she said quietly. 'And I'm guessing that a lot of people are disappointed she isn't going to be Luc's bride.'

It was a moment before Eleonora answered and when she did, her voice was fierce. 'Very disappointed,' she said bluntly. 'For it was his father's greatest wish that the Princess should marry Luc. And the Princess is as loved by the people of Mardovia as she is by her own subjects on Isolaverde.'

'I'm sure she is,' said Lisa. 'And...' Her voice tailed off. How could she possibly apologise for having ruined the plans for joining the two royal dynasties? She couldn't even say she would do her best to make up for it by being the best wife she possibly could. Not when she had every intention of withholding sex and ending the marriage just as soon as their baby was born.

So she said very little as she followed Eleonora from room to room, trying to take in the sheer scale of the place. She was shown the throne room and several reception rooms of varying degrees of splendour. There was a billiards room and a huge sports complex, with its fully equipped gym and Olympic-sized swimming pool. She peered through the arched entrance to the palace gardens and the closed door to Luc's study. *'He doesn't like anyone to disturb him in there. Only I am permitted access.'* Last of all they came to a long gallery lined with beautiful paintings, and Lisa was filled with a reluctant awe as she looked around, because this could rival some of the smaller art galleries she sometimes visited in London.

There were portraits of princes who were clearly Luc's ancestors, for they bore the same startling sapphire eyes and raven tumble of hair. There were a couple of early French Impressionists and a sombre picture of tiny matchstick men, which Lisa recognised as a Lowry. But the paintings which captured her attention were a pair hanging together in their own small section of the gallery. Luminously beautiful, both pictures depicted the same person—a woman with bobbed blonde hair. In one, she was wearing a nineteen-twenties flapper outfit with a silver headband gleaming in her pale hair, and Lisa couldn't work out if she was in fancy-dress costume or not. In the other she was flushed and smiling in a riding jacket—the tip of her crop just visible.

'Who is this?' Lisa questioned suddenly.

Eleonora's voice was cool. 'This is the Englishwoman who married one of your husband's ancestors.'

It was a curious reply to make but the coral lips were now clamped firmly closed and Lisa realised that the aide had no intention of saying any more. She sensed the guided tour was over, yet it had thrown up more questions than answers. Suddenly, the enormity of her situation hit her—the realisation of how *alien* this new world was—and for the first time since their private jet had touched down, a wave of exhaustion washed over her.

'I think I'd like to go to my room now,' she said.

'Of course. If you would like to follow me, I will show you a shortcut.'

Alone at last in the vast marital apartment, Lisa pulled off her clothes and stood beneath the luxury shower in one of the two dazzling bathrooms. Bundling her thick curls into the plastic cap she took with her everywhere, she let the powerful jets of water splash over her sticky skin and wash away some of the day's tension. Afterwards she wrapped herself in a fluffy white robe which was hanging on the bathroom door and began to explore the suite of rooms. She found an airy study, a small dining room—and floor-to-ceiling windows in the main reception room, which overlooked a garden of breathtaking beauty.

For a moment Lisa stared out at the emerald lawns and the sparkling surface of a distant lake—reflecting that it was worlds away from her home in England. Inside this vaulted room, the scent of freshly cut flowers wafted through the air and antique furniture stood on faded and exquisite silken rugs. Peeping into one of the dressing rooms, she saw that all her clothes had been neatly hung up in one of the wardrobes.

The bedroom was her last port of call and she hovered uncertainly on the threshold before going in, complicated feelings of dread and hunger washing over her as she stared at the vast bed covered with a richly embroidered throw. She didn't hear the door open or close, only realising she was no longer alone when she heard a soft sound behind her—like someone drawing in an unsteady breath—and when she turned round she saw Luc standing there.

Instantly, her mouth dried with lust and there wasn't a thing she could do about it. His hair was so black and his eyes so blue. How was it possible to want a man who had essentially trapped her here, like a prisoner? He looked so strong and powerful as he came into the bedroom that her heart began to pound in a way she wished it wouldn't, and as her breasts began to ache distractingly she said the first thing which came into her head.

'I told you I wasn't going to share a bed with you.'

He shrugged as he pulled off his jacket and draped it over the back of a gilt chair. 'It's a big bed.'

She swallowed, acutely aware of the ripple of muscle beneath his fine silk shirt. 'That's not the point.'

'No?' He tugged off his tie and tossed it on top of the jacket. 'What's the problem? You think I won't be able to refrain from touching you—or is it the other way round? Worried that you won't be able to keep your hands off me, *chérie*? Mmm…? Is that it? From the hungry look in your eyes, I'm guessing you'd like me to come right over there and get you naked.'

'In your dreams!' she spat back. 'Because even if you force me to share your bed, I shan't have sex with you, Luc, so you'd better get…get…' Her words died away as he began to undo his shirt and his glorious golden torso was laid bare, button by button. 'What…what do you think you're doing?'

'I'm undressing. What does it look like? I want to take a shower before dinner, just like you.'

'But you can't—'

'Can't what, Lisa?' The shirt had fluttered to the ground and his blue eyes gleamed as he kicked off his shoes and socks. She was rendered completely speechless by the sight of all that honed and bronzed torso before his fingers strayed suggestively to his belt. 'Does the sight of my naked body bother you?'

She told herself to look away. To look somewhere—anywhere—except at the magnificent physique which was slowly being revealed. But the trouble was that she couldn't. She was like a starving dog confronted by a large, meaty bone, which was actually the worst kind of comparison to make in the circumstances. She couldn't seem to tear her eyes away from him. He was *magnificent*, she thought as he stepped out of his trousers and she was confronted with the rock-hard reality of his powerful, hair-roughened thighs. His hips were narrow and there was an unmistakably hard ridge pushing insistently against his navy blue silk boxers—and, oh, how she longed to see the complete reveal. But she didn't dare. With a flush of embarrassment mixed with a potent sense of desire, she somehow found the courage to turn her back on him before walking over to the bed.

Heaving herself down onto the soft mattress—

her progress made slightly laborious by her swollen belly—she shut her eyes tightly but she was unable to block out the sound of Luc's mocking laughter as he headed towards the bathroom.

'Don't worry, you're quite safe from me, *chérie*,' he said softly. 'I've never found shower caps a particular turn-on.'

To Lisa's horror she realised that her curls were still squashed beneath the unflattering plastic cap, and as she heard the bathroom door close behind him she wrenched it free, shaking out her hair and lying back down on the bed again. For a while she stared up at the ceiling—at the lavish chandelier which dripped like diamonds—wishing it could be different.

But how?

Luc had married her out of duty and brought her to a place where the woman she'd usurped was infinitely more loved. How could she possibly make that right?

She must have slept, because she awoke to the smell of mint and, disorientated, opened her eyes to see Luc putting a steaming cup of tea on the table beside the bed. He had brought her *tea*?

'Feeling better?' he said.

His kindness disarmed her and she struggled to sit up, trying to ignore the ache of her breasts and the fact that he was fully dressed while she was still wearing the bathrobe which had become looser while she slept. She pulled the belt a tiny bit tighter but that only emphasised the ballooning shape of her baby bump and she silently cursed herself for caring what she looked like. At least the sight of her was unlikely to fill him with an uncontrollable lust, she reflected. It wasn't just the shower cap which wasn't a turn-on, it was everything about her...

She cleared her throat. 'Much better, thanks,' she lied. 'What time is dinner?'

Luc walked over to the window and watched as she began to sip at her tea. With her face all flushed and her hair mussed, she looked strangely vulnerable—as if she was too sleepy to have remembered to wear her familiar mask of defiance. Right then it would have been so easy to take her into his arms and kiss away some of the unmistakable tension which made her body look so brittle. But she'd made her desires clear—or, rather, the lack of them. She didn't want intimacy and, although right now he sensed she might be open to *persuasion*, it wouldn't work in his favour if he put her in a position which afterwards she regretted. And she was *pregnant*, he reminded himself. She was carrying his baby and therefore she deserved his consideration and protection.

'Dinner is whenever you want it to be.'

She put the cup back down on the saucer, looking a little uncomfortable. 'Will it be served in that huge room with all the golden plates?'

'You mean the formal banqueting room which we use for state functions? I don't tend to eat most meals in there,' he added drily. 'There are smaller and less intimidating rooms we can use.' He paused. 'Or I could always have them bring you something here, on a tray.'

'Seriously? You mean like a TV dinner?' Her green-gold eyes widened. 'Won't people think it odd if we don't go down?'

'I am the Prince and you are my wife and we can do whatever we damned well like,' he said arrogantly. 'What would you like to eat?'

'I know it probably sounds stupid, but I'd love… well, what I'd like more than anything is an egg sandwich.' She looked up at him from between her lashes. 'Do you think that's possible?'

He gave a short laugh. When she looked at him like that, he felt as if anything were possible. But how ironic that the only woman in a position to ask for anything should have demanded something so fundamentally *humble*. 'I think that can be arranged.'

A uniformed servant answered his summons, soon reappearing with the sandwich she'd wanted—most of which she devoured with an uninhibited hunger which Luc found curiously sensual. Or maybe it was the fact that she was ignoring him which had stirred his senses—because he wasn't used to *that* either.

After she'd finished and put her napkin down, she looked up at him, her face suddenly serious.

'Eleonora showed me the gallery today,' she said.

'Good. I wanted you to see as much of the palace as possible.'

She traced a figure of eight on the linen tablecloth with the tip of her finger before looking up.

'I noticed two paintings of the same woman. Beautiful paintings—in a specially lit section of the gallery.'

He nodded. 'Yes. Two of Kristjan Wheeler's finest works. Conall Devlin acquired one of them for me.'

'Yes, I knew he was an art dealer as well as a property tycoon,' she said. 'But what I was wondering was...'

He set down his glass of red wine as her voice tailed off. 'What?' he questioned coolly.

She wriggled her shoulders and her hazelnut curls shimmered. 'Why Eleonora seemed so *cagey* when I asked about the paintings.'

He shrugged. 'Eleonora has always been the most loyal of all my aides.'

'How lovely for you,' she said politely. 'But surely as your wife I am expected to know—'

'Who she is? The woman in the paintings?' he

finished as he picked up his glass and swirled the burgundy liquid around the bowl-like shape of the glass. 'She was an Englishwoman called Louisa De Lacy, who holidayed here during the early part of the last century. She was an unconventional woman—an adventuress was how she liked to style herself. A crack shot who smoked cheroots and wore dresses designed to shock.'

'And is that relevant? She sounds fun.'

'Very relevant. Mardovia was under the rule of one of my ancestors and he fell madly in love with her. The trouble was that Miss De Lacy wasn't deemed suitable on any grounds, even if she'd wanted to be a princess, which she didn't. Despite increasing opposition, he refused to give her up and eventually he was forced to renounce the throne and was exiled from Mardovia. After his abdication his younger brother took the crown— my great-great-grandfather—and that is how it came to be passed down to me.'

'And was that a problem?' she questioned curiously.

He shrugged. 'Not for me. Not even for my father—because we were born knowing we must rule—but for my great-great-grandfather, yes. He had never wanted to govern and was married to a woman who was painfully shy. The burden of the crown contributed to his early death, for which his wife never forgave Louisa De Lacy, and in the meantime…'

'In the meantime, what?' she whispered as his voice trailed off.

'Unfortunately the exiled Prince was killed in a riding accident before he could marry Louisa, who by then had given birth to his child.'

Her head jerked up. 'You mean…'

Luc's temper suddenly shortened. Maybe it was because he was tired and frustrated. Because she was sitting there with that cascade of curls flowing down over her engorged breasts and he wanted to make love to her. He wanted to explore her luscious body with fingers which were on the verge of trembling with frustration, not to have to sit here recounting his family history. Because this was not the wedding night he had anticipated.

'I mean that somewhere out there a child was born out of wedlock—a child of royal Mardovian blood who was never seen again—and they say that there is none so dangerous as a dispossessed prince.' His voice grew hard. 'And I was not prepared for history to repeat itself. Because I have no brothers, Lisa. No one else to pass on the reins to, should I fail to produce an heir. Succession is vital to me, and to my land.'

'So that's why you forced me to marry you,' she breathed.

He nodded. It was not the whole truth, but it

was part of it—because he was slowly coming to realise that there were worse fates than having a woman like Lisa by his side. Duty, yes—he would not shirk from that—but couldn't duty be clothed in pleasure?

Wasn't she aware that now he had her here, he had no intention of letting her or the child go? If she accepted that with a good grace then so much the better, but accept it she would. His will was stronger than hers and he would win because he *always* won.

And then something else occurred to him—a fact which he had pushed to the back of his mind because the sheer logistics of getting her here had consumed all his thoughts. But it was something he needed to address sooner rather than later. He tensed as he realised that until they consummated the marriage, their union was not legal. His heart missed a beat. He realised that, but did she?

He remembered her defiant words on the plane—a variation on what she'd said just now, when she'd announced she had no intention of sharing a bed with him. He didn't doubt her resolve, not for a moment, for Lisa was a strong and proud woman. Yet women were capricious creatures who could have their minds changed for them. But only if you played them carefully. He had learnt his first lessons in female manipulation from the governesses who'd been employed to look after him after his mother's death. Run after a woman and it gave her power. Act like you didn't care and she would be yours for the taking.

Duty clothed in pleasure.

He had vowed to be a good husband as well as a good father, so surely one of his responsibilities was making sure his wife received an adequate share of sexual satisfaction? He looked at her green-gold eyes and as he detected the glint of sexual hunger she could not disguise, he smiled.

His for the taking.

CHAPTER EIGHT

THE NEXT FEW weeks were so full with being a new wife, a new princess *and* mother-to-be that Lisa had barely any time to get homesick. Eleonora introduced her to most of the palace staff, to her own personal driver and the two protection officers who would accompany her whenever she left the palace. She was given her own special servant—Almeera—a quiet, dark-eyed beauty who chattered excitedly about how much she loved babies. She met the royal dressmaker who said she'd happily make up Lisa's own designs for the duration of her pregnancy, or they could send to Paris or London for any couture requirements the Princess might have.

She also had her first appointment with the palace obstetrician, Dr Gautier, who came to examine her in her royal apartments, accompanied by a midwife. At least Eleonora made herself scarce for that particular appointment, although Lisa was surprised when Luc made a sudden appearance just before the consultation began.

Her heart began to pound as he walked into the room, nodding to the doctor and midwife who had stood up to bow, before coming to sit beside her and giving her hand a reassuring squeeze. And even though she knew the gesture was mainly for the benefit of the watching medics, she stupidly *felt* reassured. Could he feel the thunder of her pulse? Was he aware that her breasts started to ache whenever he was close? She wondered if they looked like any other newly-wed couple from the outside and what the doctor would say if he realised they hadn't had sex since the night their child was conceived. And she wondered what Luc would say if he knew how at night she lay there, wide-eyed in the dark—unable to sleep because her body was craving his expert touch...

Dr Gautier flicked through the file which lay on the desk before him before fixing his eyes firmly on Luc.

'I am assuming that Your Royal Highness already knows the sex of the baby?' he questioned.

Did Luc hear Lisa's intake of breath? All he had to do was to ask the doctor what he wanted to know and it would be done. The fact would be out there. Lisa swallowed. Some people might think she was being awkward in not wanting this particular piece of information, but it was important to her. It felt like her last remnant of independence and the only control she had left over her life.

'My wife doesn't wish to know,' said Luc, meeting her eyes with a faintly mocking expression. 'She wants it to be a surprise on the day.'

'Very sensible,' said the doctor, turning to ask Lisa if there was anything she wanted to know.

The questions she wanted to ask were not for the obstetrician's ears. Nor for the ears of the husband sitting beside her.

How soon can I return to England after the birth? When will Luc let me leave him?

Or the most troubling of all.

Will I ever stop wanting a man who sees me only as the vessel which carries his child?

But some of Lisa's fears left her that day and she wasn't sure why. Was it Luc's simple courtesy in not demanding to know the sex of their baby? Or that meaningless little squeeze of her hand which had made her relax her defences a little? Afterwards, when they were back in their suite, she turned to him to thank him and the baby chose that moment to deliver a hefty kick just beneath her ribs. Automatically, she winced before smiling as she clutched her stomach and when she looked into Luc's face, she was surprised by the sudden *longing* she read in his eyes.

She asked the question because she knew she had to, pushing aside the thought that it was a somehow dangerous thing to do—to invite him to touch her. 'Would you like to…to feel the baby kick?'

'May I?'

She nodded, holding her breath as he laid his hand over her belly and they waited for the inevitable propulsion of one tiny foot. She heard him laugh in disbelief as a tiny heel connected with his palm and, once the movement had subsided, she wondered if he would now do what her body was longing for him to do—and continue touching her in a very different way. She thought how easy it would be. He could move his hand upwards to cup a painfully engorged breast and slowly caress her nipple with the pad of his thumb. Or downwards, to slide his fingers between her legs and find how hot and hungry she was for him.

But he didn't.

He removed his hand from her belly and although she silently cursed and wanted to draw him back to her, she was in no position to do so. She wondered if she had been too hasty in rejecting him, particularly when she hadn't realised he could be so *kind*. And she was fast discovering that kindness could be as seductive as any kiss.

Maybe that was the turning point for Lisa. The discovery that as the days passed the palace stopped feeling like a prison. Or maybe it was a direct result of Luc's sudden announcement that he had a surprise for her. One morning after breakfast, he led her through the endless maze of corridors to a part of the palace she hadn't seen before, where he opened a set of double doors, before beckoning her inside.

'Come and take a look at this,' he said. 'And tell me what you think.'

Lisa was momentarily lost for words as she walked into an airy studio overlooking the palace gardens. She glanced around, trying to take it all in—because in it was everything a dress designer could ever desire. On a big desk were pencils and paints and big pads of sketch paper. There was a computer, a sophisticated music system, a tiny kitchen and even a TV.

'For when you get bored,' Luc drawled. 'I wasn't sure if artwork on the walls would inspire you or distract you—but if you'd like some paintings, then speak to Eleonora and she'll arrange for you to have something from the palace collection.' He searched her face with quizzical eyes. 'I hope this meets with your satisfaction?'

It was a long time since anyone had done something so thoughtful. Something just for *her* and Lisa felt overwhelmed—a feeling compounded by the way Luc was looking at her. His skin was glowing and his black hair was still ruffled from the horse ride he liked to take before breakfast each morning. Which she guessed explained why he was never there when she woke up. Why on more than one occasion she'd found herself rolling over to encounter nothing but a cool space where his warm body should have been.

Because he had spoken the truth. It *was* a big bed. Big enough for two people to share it without touching. For them to lie side by side like two strangers. For her to be acutely aware of his nakedness, even though she couldn't actually see it. Yet as the dark minutes of the night ticked by— punctuated only by the rhythmical sounds of Luc's steady breathing—Lisa was furious with herself for *wanting* him to make love to her. Wondering why hadn't he even *tried* to change her mind? Was her swollen belly putting him off? More than once she had wondered what he would do if she silently moved to his side of the bed. She could put her hand between his legs and start to caress him in that way he liked. She swallowed. Actually, she had a pretty good idea what he'd do...

'I love it,' she said softly, cheeks flushing with embarrassment at her erotic thoughts as she lifted her gaze from the pencils lined up with military precision. 'Thank you.'

There was a pause as their eyes met. An infinitesimal pause when Lisa thought she saw his mouth relax. A moment when his eyes hinted at that flinty look they used to get just before he kissed her. She held her breath. Hoping. No, praying. Thinking—to hell with all her supposedly noble intentions. He was her husband, wasn't he? He was her husband and right then she wanted him with a hunger which was tearing through her body like wildfire. He could make love to her right now—she was sure he would be gentle with her. She felt the molten ache of frustration as she imagined him touching her where she was crying out to be touched.

But just like always, he moved away from her. Only by a fraction, but it might as well have been a mile. She found her cheeks growing even pinker; she walked over to one of the pristine drawing pads in an effort to distract herself. 'I'll start work on my next collection right away,' she said.

He turned to leave but at the door, he paused. 'Has Eleonora told you about the May Ball?'

Lisa shook her head. No. That was something Eleonora must have missed during daily conversations, which usually managed to convey how matey Princess Sophie's father had been with Luc's father, and about the blissful holidays the two families used to enjoy on the island of Isolaverde.

'No,' she said slowly. 'I don't believe she did. Anyway, shouldn't it have been you who told me?'

He raised his eyebrows. 'I'm telling you now,' he said, with a trace of his customary arrogance. 'It's something of a palace tradition. The weather is always fine and the gardens are at their loveliest. It will be the perfect opportunity for you to meet the great and the good. Oh, and you might want to wear some jewels from the royal collection. Speak to Eleonora and she'll show you.'

Lisa forced a smile. She seemed to do nothing but *speak to Eleonora*, but she nodded her head in agreement. And after Luc had gone, she emailed her sister and asked for some new photos of Tamsin, before taking herself off into the palace grounds for a walk.

The gardens were exquisite. Not just the rose section or the intricate maze which led onto the biggest herb garden she'd ever seen, but there were also high-hedged walkways where you could suddenly turn a corner and find some gorgeous marble statue hidden away. Yet today Lisa had to work hard to focus on the beauty of her surroundings because all she could think about was Luc's attitude towards her. He could do something immensely kind and thoughtful like surprising her with a new studio or bring her tea in bed, but he seemed content to keep her at arm's length and push her in the direction of his ever-loyal Eleonora.

But that was what she had wanted.

Only now she was beginning to realise she didn't want it any more. She didn't want to lie chastely by his side while he slept and her body hungered for him. She wanted him to take her in his arms and kiss her. If not to love her—then at least to *make* love to her. Suddenly, withholding sex as a kind of bargaining tool seemed not only stupid, but self-sacrificing. Maybe she had misjudged the whole situation. She wanted the freedom to be able to return to England but she recognised that she needed Luc's blessing in order to do so. Wouldn't he be more amenable to reason if he was physically satisfied?

And wouldn't she?

He had told her about the ball and he wanted her to wear some of the royal jewels. Couldn't she embrace her new role as his princess and appear comfortable in it? Wouldn't he be pleasantly pleased—maybe even proud of her—giving her the perfect opportunity to seduce him? And since Luc showed no sign of coming on to *her*, she was going to have to be proactive. If she wanted him, then she must show him how much…

She felt the baby stirring inside her, almost as if it were giving her the proverbial thumbs-up, and Lisa felt a sudden warmth creep through her veins. Fired up by a new resolve, she made her way back towards the palace, sunlight streaming onto her bare head. Going straight to her studio, she rang for Eleonora and the aide arrived almost immediately, a questioning look on her smooth face.

Lisa drew a deep breath. 'Luc told me about the ball. He suggested I might wear some of the crown jewels for the occasion.'

Eleonora gave a bland smile. 'Indeed. He has already mentioned it to me.'

Lisa didn't miss a beat, squashing down her indignation. Didn't matter that he confided in Eleonora, because soon he would be in *her* arms and confiding in *her*. 'Could we go and take a look at them, please? Now? Because I think I'd like to design my outfit around the jewels.'

'Of course.'

The collection was housed in a section of the palace not far from the art gallery, and Lisa was momentarily startled when she walked into the spot-lighted room, where priceless gems sparkled against inky backdrops of black velvet. Her eyes widened at the sheer opulence of the pieces on display. There were glittering waterfalls of diamonds—white ones and pink ones and even citrusy yellow ones, some with matching drop earrings and bracelets. There were sapphires as blue as Luc's eyes and mysterious milky opals, shot through with rainbows. Lisa was just about to choose a choker of square-cut emeralds when Eleonora indicated a set of drawers at the far end of the room.

'How about these?' Eleonora suggested softly, pulling open one of the drawers and beckoning for Lisa to take a closer look.

Lisa blinked. Inside was a flamboyant ruby necklace with glittering stones as big as gulls' eggs—their claret colour highlighted by the white fire of surrounding diamonds.

'Oh, my word,' she breathed. 'That is the most exquisite thing I've ever seen.'

'Isn't it just?' agreed Eleonora softly as she carefully removed the necklace. 'It hasn't been worn for a long time and is probably the most valuable piece in our entire collection. Why not surprise your husband with it?'

The jewels spilled like rich wine over Lisa's fingers as she took them from the aide, and she could picture exactly the kind of dress to wear with them.

It became a labour of love. Something to work towards. Making her dress for the ball became her secret and she decided it would be her gift to Luc. An olive branch handed to him to make him realise she was prepared to do things differently from now on. That the current situation was far from satisfactory and she'd like to change it. She wanted to be his lover as well as his wife.

'You are looking very pleased with yourself of late,' he observed one evening as they walked down the wide marble corridor towards the dining room.

'Am I?'

'Mmm.' His gaze roved over her as a servant opened the doors for them. 'Actually, you look... *blooming*.'

'Thank you.' She smiled at him. 'I think that's how pregnant women are supposed to look.'

Luc inclined his head in agreement, waiting until she'd sat down before taking his seat opposite and observing her remarkable transformation. When she'd first arrived she had looked strung out and her expression had been pinched—something which had not been improved by their unsatisfactory sleeping arrangements. He had briefly considered moving into his old bachelor rooms to give her the peace she so obviously needed. To make her realise that the only thing worse than sharing a bed with him was *not* sharing a bed with him.

But then some miraculous thaw had occurred. Suddenly, she seemed almost…contented. He heard her humming as she brushed her teeth before bed. He noticed that she'd started reading the Mardovian history book he had given her on the plane. Hungrily, he had watched the luscious thrust of her breasts as she walked into the bedroom with a silken nightdress clinging to every ripe curve of her body, and realised he had nobody but himself to blame for his frustration. He could feel himself growing hard beneath the sheets and had to quickly lie on his belly, willing his huge erection to go away, and he wondered if now was the time to make a move on her. Because his experience with women told him that she would welcome him with open arms…

'You are excited about the ball?' he questioned one evening when they were finishing dinner.

'I'm…looking forward to it.'

His eyes flicked over her. 'You have something to wear?'

'You mean…' on the opposite side of the table she smoothed her hand down over the curve of her belly '…something which will fit over my ever-expanding girth? It's not very attractive, is it?'

'If you really want to know, I find it very attractive,' he said huskily.

She stilled, her hand remaining exactly where it was. 'You don't have to say that just to make me feel better.'

'I never say anything I don't mean.' He touched the tip of his tongue to his lips to help ease their aching dryness and wished it were as simple to relieve the aching in his groin. 'So why don't you go and put on your dress? Show me what you'll be wearing.'

She hesitated. 'It's a secret.'

For some reason her words jarred, or maybe it was his apparent misreading of the situation. The idea that she was softening towards him a little— only to be met with that same old brick wall of resistance.

'So many secrets,' he mocked.

At this her smile died.

'That's a bit rich, coming from the master of

secrecy,' she said. 'There's so much about your-self that you keep locked away, Luc. And, of course, there's the biggest concealment of all. If you hadn't kept your fiancée such a big *secret*, we wouldn't have found ourselves in this situa-tion, would we?'

'And doubtless you would have preferred that?'

'Wouldn't you?'

Her challenge fell between them like a stone dropped into a well but Luc told himself he would not allow himself to be trapped into answering hypothetical questions. Instead, he deflected her anger with a careless question. 'What is it about the hidden me you would like revealed, my princess?'

She put down the pearl-handled knife with which she had been peeling an apple and he won-dered how deeply she would pry. Whether she would want him to divulge the dark night of his soul to her—and if he did, would that make her understand why he could never really be the man she needed?

'What was it like for you, growing up here?'

It was an innocent enough query but Luc re-alised too late that all questions were a form of en-trapment. That if you gave someone an answer, it paved the way for more questions and more expo-sure. He gave a bland smile, the type he had used countless times in diplomatic debate. He would not lie to her. No. He would be… What was it that accountants sometimes said? Ah, yes. He would be economical with the truth.

'I imagine it was the same for me as for many other princes born into palaces and surrounded by unimaginable riches,' he said. 'There is always someone to do your bidding and I never wanted for anything.'

Except love, of course.

'Whatever I asked for, I was given.'

But never real companionship.

'I was schooled with other Mardovian aristocrats until the age of eighteen, when I went to school in Paris.'

Where he had tasted freedom for the first time in his life and found it irresistible. But the truth was that nothing had ever been able to fill the emptiness at the very core of him.

'And what about your mum and dad?'

Luc flinched. He had never heard his royal parents described quite so informally, and his first instinct was to correct her and ask her to refer to them by their titles. But he slapped his instinct down, because a lesson in palace protocol would not serve him well at this moment. Not when she was looking at him with that unblinking gaze which was making his heart clench with something he didn't recognise.

'Like you, my mother died when I was very young.'

'I'm sorry for your loss,' she said instantly and there was a pause. 'Did your father remarry?'

He shook his head. 'No.' His father had been locked in his own private world of grief—oblivious to the fact that a small boy was hurting and desperately missing his mother. Unable to look at the child who so resembled his dead wife, he had channelled that grief into duty—pouring all his broken-hearted passion into serving his country. And leaving the care of his son to the stream of governesses employed to look after him.

'I don't think he considered anyone could ever take the place of my mother,' he continued slowly and he felt a twist of pain. Because hadn't he witnessed his father's emotional dependence on the woman who had died—and hadn't it scared him to see such a powerful person diminished by the bitterness of heartbreak?

'How old were you?'

'Four,' he said flatly.

'So who looked after you?'

'Governesses.' Even the sound of the word sent shivers down his spine as he thought of those fierce women, so devoted to his father—who had put duty to the throne above everything else. They had taught him never to cry. Never to show weakness, or fear. They had taught him that a prince must sublimate his own desires in order to best serve his country.

'What were they like?'

He considered Lisa's question—about how many countless variations there were on the word *cold*. 'Efficient,' he said eventually.

She smiled a little. 'That doesn't tell me very much.'

'Maybe it wasn't supposed to.'

But still she persisted. 'And did they show you lots of affection?'

And this, he realised, was an impossible question to answer except with the baldness of truth. 'None whatsoever,' he said slowly. 'There were several of them on some sort of rotation and I think it must have been agreed that they should treat me politely and carefully. I don't think it was intended for any of them to become a mother substitute, or for me to attach myself to anyone in particular. I suspect there was a certain amount of competitiveness between them and they were unwilling to tolerate me having a favourite.'

'Oh, Luc.' Did she notice his faint frown, intended to discourage further questioning? Was that why she deliberately brightened her tone?

'You were lucky,' she added. 'At least you didn't have the proverbial wicked stepmother to deal with.'

He looked into her eyes. Was he? Was anyone ever really 'lucky'? You worked with what you had and fashioned fate to suit you.

He sensed she was softening towards him and that filled him with satisfaction. He had played his part with his restraint—now let her play hers. Let her admit that she wanted him. He gave a grim smile.

Because you made your own luck in life.

CHAPTER NINE

THE MAY BALL was the biggest event in the palace calendar, and Lisa planned her first formal introduction to the people of Mardovia with the precision of a military campaign. She ordered a bolt of crimson silk satin and made a gown specially designed to showcase the ruby and diamond necklace from the royal collection.

For hours she worked to the familiar and comforting sound of the sewing machine, painstakingly finishing off the gown with some careful hand stitching. She would surprise Luc with her dress, yes. Her pulse began to race. And not just at the ball. Her self-imposed sex ban had gone on for long enough and now she wanted him in her arms again. He had heeded her words and treated her with respect. Night after night he had lain beside her without attempting to touch her—even though there had been times when she'd wished he would. When that slow heat would build low in her belly, making her want to squirm with frustration as he slept beside her.

She finished the dress to her satisfaction but as she got ready for the ball she felt shot with nerves—because what if Luc had decided he no longer wanted her? What if their stand-off had killed his desire for her? Smoothing down the full-length skirt, she stared at her reflected image in the mirror. He *had* to want her.

She thought back to how she'd felt when she had first arrived here, when she'd married him under duress and had been apprehensive about what lay ahead. But he had respected her wishes and not touched her. And as he had gradually opened up to her, so had her fears about the future diminished. For fear had no place in the heart of a mother-to-be and neither did selfishness. The life she had been prepared to embrace now seemed all wrong. She'd thought a lot about Luc's lonely childhood and the repercussions of that. And she knew she couldn't subject this baby to single parenthood without first giving her husband the chance to be a full-time father. *And a full-time husband.*

Her heart began thundering with an emotion she could no longer deny. Because when tonight's ball was ended, she was going to take her husband in her arms and tell him she wanted them to start over. Tell him she was willing to try to create the kind of family unit which neither of them had ever had before. And then she was going to seduce him…

The woman in the mirror looked back at her with hope shining from her eyes and Lisa allowed herself a small smile. Years of working in the fashion industry had taught her to be impartial—especially about her own appearance. She knew that her already curvy body was swollen with child but she was also aware that never had she looked quite so radiant as she did tonight. Her hair was glossy and her skin was glowing. Her handmade dress was fitted tightly on the bodice and cleverly pleated at the front, so that it fell to the ground in a flattering silhouette. And the stark, square neckline provided the perfect setting for the real star of the show— the royal rubies which blazed like fire against her pale skin.

'Lisa!'

She heard Luc calling and, picking up the full-length black velvet cloak lined with matching crimson satin, she slipped it around her shoulders. Luc would see her at the same time as all his subjects and friends, she thought happily. Tonight she was going to *do him proud*.

'Nervous?' he questioned as she walked alongside him through the flame-lit corridors in a rustle of velvet and silk.

'A little,' she admitted.

He glanced down at the dramatic fall of black velvet which covered her entire body. 'Aren't you going to show me this dress you've been working on so furiously?'

'I will when we get there.'

'Are you hiding your bump until the last minute? Is that it?'

'Partly.' Lisa felt the heavy necklace brushing against her throat and shivered a little as she pulled the cloak closer. 'And I'm a little cold.'

But it wasn't just nerves which were making her skin prickle with little goosebumps, because the fine weather which traditionally characterised the May Ball hadn't materialised. As soon as Lisa had opened her eyes that morning, she'd realised something was different. For the first time since she'd been on the island, the sun wasn't shining and the air was laced with an unseasonable chill. According to the servant who had served her breakfast, the temperamental wind they called Il Serpente was threatening to wreak havoc on the Mediterranean island.

But although the predinner drinks had now been moved inside, the palace looked more magnificent than Lisa had ever seen it. Dark roses threaded into ivy were woven around the tall ballroom pillars, giving the place a distinctly gothic feel, and more crimson roses decorated the long table where the meal would be served. The string section of the Mardovian orchestra was playing softly, but as soon as the trumpets announced her and Luc's arrival they burst into the national anthem. As the stirring tune drew to a close, Lisa slipped the velvet cloak from her shoulders.

She was not expecting such an OTT reaction as the collective gasps from the guests who had assembled to greet the royal guests of honour. Nor for her to glance up into Luc's face to find herself startled by the dark look stamped onto his features which seemed to echo the growing storm outside. Was her dress a mistake? Did the vibrant colour draw attention to the swell of her body, reminding the Prince and all his subjects of the real reason she was here?

'Is something…wrong?'

Luc's cold gaze was fixed on the blaze of jewels at her throat, but he must have been aware that everyone around them was listening because he curved his lips into a smile which did not meet his eyes. 'Wrong?' he questioned smoothly. 'Why should there be anything wrong? You look exquisite. Utterly exquisite, *ma chérie*.'

But Lisa didn't feel exquisite as she sat down to dinner, in front of all that shiny golden cutlery. She felt *tawdry*. As if she'd broken a fundamental rule which nobody had bothered to tell her about. What on earth was the matter? And then she glanced down the table and met Eleonora's eyes and wondered if she was imagining the brief look of triumph which passed over the aide's face.

Somehow she managed to get through the lavish meal, perversely relieved that protocol meant she wasn't sitting next to her husband, because no way could she have eaten a thing if she'd been forced to endure another second of his inexplicable rage. She had lost her appetite anyway and merely picked at her food as she tried to respond to the Sultan of Qurhah's amusing observations, when all she could think about was Luc's forbidding posture. But it wasn't until the dancing started and he came over to lead her imperiously onto the ballroom floor for the first dance that she found herself alone with him at last.

'Something *is* wrong,' she hissed as he slid his arms around her waist, but instead of it being a warm embrace, it felt as if she were locked inside a powerful vice. 'Isn't it? You've been glaring at me all evening. Luc, what's the matter? What am I supposed to have *done*?'

'Not here,' he bit out. 'I'm not having this discussion here.'

'Then why are you bothering to dance with me?'

'Because you are my wife and I must be *seen*

to dance with you.' His words were like ice. 'To paint the illusion of marital bliss for my idealistic subjects. That is why.'

Distress welled up inside her and Lisa wanted to push him away from her. To flounce from the ballroom with her head held high so that nobody could see the glimmer of tears which were pricking at the backs of her eyes. But pride wouldn't let her. She mustn't give anyone the opportunity to brand her as some kind of hysteric. That would be a convenient category for a woman like her, wouldn't it?

So she closed her eyes to avoid having to look at her husband and as she danced woodenly in his arms, she wondered how she could have been so stupid. Had she really thought that some silent truce had been declared between them? That they had reached a cautious kind of harmony?

Stupid Lisa, she thought bitterly. She had let it happen all over again. Despite everything she knew to be true, she had allowed herself to trust him. She had started to imagine a marriage they might be able to work at. A marriage which might just succeed.

Behind her tightly shut eyelids she willed away her tears and finished her dance with Luc, and afterwards she danced with the Sultan and then the cousin of the Sheikh of Jazratan. Somehow she managed to play the part expected of her, even though her smile felt as if it had been plastered to her lips like concrete.

But at least her late pregnancy gave her a solid reason to excuse herself early. She slipped away from the ballroom and had one of the servants bring her cloak, which she wrapped tightly around herself as she made her way back along the deserted corridors to their apartments.

Once inside the suite, she didn't bother putting the lights on. She stood at the window and watched as the storm split open the skies. Forked lightning streaked like an angry silver weapon against the menacing clouds and the sound of thunder was almost deafening. But after a while she didn't even see the elemental raging outside because the tears which were streaming down her face made her vision blurry. She dashed them away with an impatient hand, unsure of what to do next. Should she get ready for bed? Yet wouldn't lying on that monstrous mattress in her nightgown make her even more vulnerable than she already felt?

So she rang for some camomile tea and had just finished drinking it when the doors were flung open and the silhouetted form of her husband stood on the threshold. He was breathing heavily and his body was hard and tense as he stared inside the room. She could tell that he was trying to adjust his vision to the dim light, but when he reached out to put on one of the lamps, she snapped out a single word.

'Don't.'

'You like sitting in the dark?'

'There's nothing I particularly *like* right now, Luc. But somewhere near the top of my dislikes is having you try to control the situation yet again. If anyone's going to put the light on, it's going to be me. Understand?' She snapped on the nearest lamp, steeling herself against the sight of his powerful body in the immaculate dress suit as he shut the door behind him with a shaking hand. And even though she felt the betraying stir of her senses, her anger was far more powerful than her desire. 'Do you want to tell me what I've done wrong?' she demanded. 'What heinous crime I'm supposed to have committed?'

She could see the tension in his body increase and when he spoke, his words sounded as if they had been chipped from a block of ice. 'Why the hell did you wear that necklace without running it past me first?'

For a moment she blinked in surprise. Because he'd told her to choose some jewels from the royal collection. Because Eleonora had drawn her attention to the undoubted star of the collection and quietly suggested that she 'surprise' her husband.

Lisa opened her mouth to tell him that, but suddenly her curiosity was piqued. 'I didn't realise I had to *run it past* you first. You made no mention of any kind of *vetting* procedure. What was wrong with me wearing it?'

There was a pause as his face became shuttered and still his words were icy-cold. 'That necklace was given to my mother by Princess Sophie's mother. My mother wore it on her wedding day. It was—'

'It was supposed to be worn by Sophie on the day of her marriage to you,' finished Lisa dully, her heart clenching. 'Only you never married her, like you were supposed to do. You married a stranger. A commoner. A woman heavy with your child who appeared at the ball tonight looking like some spectre at the feast. The wrong woman wearing the jewels.'

Her remarks were greeted by silence, but what could he possibly say? He could hardly deny the truth. Lisa ran her tongue over her lips. She supposed she could tell him it had been Eleonora's subtle lead which had made her choose the rubies, but what good would that do? She would be like a child in the classroom, telling tales to the teacher. And it wouldn't change the facts, would it? That she was like a cuckoo in the nest with no real place here. An outsider who would always be

just that. The human incubator who carried the
royal heir. Reaching up, she unclipped the necklace and pulled it from her neck, dropping it down
onto a bureau so that it fell there in a spooling clat-
ter of gems.

But as her anger bubbled up, so did something
else—a powerful wave of frustration, fuelled by
the sudden violent see-sawing of her hormones.
For weeks now she'd been trying her best to fit
in with this strange new life of hers. Night after
night she had lain by his side, staring up at the
ceiling while he had fallen into a deep sleep. She
had been polite to the servants and tried to learn
everything she could about Mardovia—only now
he was treating her with all the contempt he might
have reserved for some passing tramp who had
stumbled uninvited into his royal apartment. How
dared he? How *dared* he?

'Well, damn you, Luc Leonidas!' she cried, and
she launched herself across the room and began to
batter her fists hard against his chest. 'Damn you
to high heaven!'

At first he tried to halt her by imprisoning her
wrists, but that only made her kick even harder
at his shins and he uttered something soft and el-
oquent in French—before swooping his mouth
down on hers.

His kiss was hard—and *angry*—but his probing tongue met no resistance from her. On the contrary, it made her give a shuddering little moan of something like recognition—because she could do anger, too. So she kissed him back just as hard, even though he was now trying to pull away from her, something impossible to achieve when he was still holding her wrists. And then his grip on her loosened and she took that opportunity to stroke her fingertip down his cheek and then over the rasp of his chin. And although he shook his head when she continued down over his chest, he didn't stop her—not until her hand reached his groin, where he was so hard for her that her body stiffened in anticipation.

'Lisa, no,' he warned unsteadily as she slid her palm over the rocky ridge beneath his trousers.

'Luc, *yes*,' she mimicked as she began to slide down the protesting zip.

After that there was no turning back. Nothing but urgent and hungry kissing as she freed his erection and gazed down at it with wide-eyed pleasure. But when she began to slide her finger and thumb up and down over the silken shaft, he batted her hand away then picked her up and carried her over to the bed. He set her down beside it, his eyes flicking over the long line of hooks which went all the way down the back of her dress, and his hands were shaking as he reached for the first.

'No,' she said, wriggling away from him as she pushed him down onto the bed. 'It will take too long and I'm done with waiting. I'm not going to wait a second longer for this.' With an air of determination, she began to tug off his trousers and boxer shorts, before slithering out of her panties and climbing on top of him, uncaring of her bulkiness. Not caring that this was wrong—because the powerful hunger which was pulsing through her body was blotting out everything but desire.

'Lisa…' His words sounded slurred and husky as her bare flesh brushed against his. He swallowed. 'We can't…we can't do this.'

'Oh, but we can. There are many things we can't do, but this isn't one of them.' The red silk dress ballooned around her as she positioned herself over him, and she saw his eyes grow smoky as the tip of him began to push insistently against her wet heat.

'But you're…pregnant,' he breathed.

'You think I don't know that?' She gave a hollow laugh. 'You think pregnant women don't have sex? Then I put it to you that you, Luc Leonidas, with all your supposed experience of the female body, are very wrong.' Slowly she lowered herself down onto his steely shaft, biting out a gasp as that first rush of pleasure hit her.

He lay there perfectly still as she began to rock forward and back and she could see the almost helpless look of desire on his face as her bulky body accustomed itself to the movements. And she *liked* seeing him like that. Powerful Prince Luc at *her* mercy. But her sense of victory only lasted until the first shimmerings of pleasure began to ripple over her body and then, of course, he took over. His hands anchored to her hips, he angled his own to increase the level of penetration while leaning forward to whisper soft little kisses over her satin-covered belly. And it was that which was her undoing. That which made her heart melt. His stupid show of tenderness which *didn't mean a thing*.

Not a thing.

All it did was make her long for the impossible. For Luc to love her and want her and need her. And that was never going to happen.

But she could do nothing to stop the orgasm which caught her up and dragged her under, and as her body began to convulse around him she heard his own ragged groan. His arms tightened as he held her against him, his lips buried in the hard swell of her stomach as he kissed it, over and over again. For a while there was nothing but contentment as Lisa clung to him, listening to the muffled pounding of her heart.

But not for long. Once the pleasure began to ebb away, she forced herself to pull away from him, collapsing back against the pile of pillows and deliberately turning her face to the wall as a deep sense of shame washed over her. How could she? How *could* she have done that? Climbed on top of him with that out-of-control and wanton desire?

'Lisa?'

She felt the warmth of his hand as he placed it over one tense shoulder and some illogical part of her wanted to sink back into his embrace and stay there. Because when he touched her it felt as if all the things she didn't believe in had come true. It felt like love. *And she couldn't afford to think that way because love was nothing but an illusion.* Especially with Luc.

She closed her eyes as she pushed his hand away, because she was through with illusions. With going back on everything she knew to be true and allowing herself to get sucked into fantasy. He was a man, wasn't he? And no man could really be trusted. Did she need someone to carve it on a metal disc for her, so she could wear it around her neck? She needed to be strong enough to resist him and, for that, she needed him to go.

'Lisa?' Luc said again and his ragged sigh ruffled the curls at the back of her neck. 'Look, I know I overreacted about the necklace and I'm sorry.'

She pulled away. 'It doesn't matter.'

'It *does* matter.'

But she wasn't in the mood to listen. She made

herself yawn as she curled up into a ball—well, as much of a ball as her heavily pregnant state would allow. 'I just want to go to sleep,' she mumbled. 'And I'd prefer to do it alone.'

CHAPTER TEN

'LISA, WE HAVE to talk about this. We can't keep pretending nothing has happened.'

Lisa closed her eyes as Luc's voice washed over her skin, its rich tone setting her senses tingling the way it always did. It made her think of things she was trying to forget. Things she *needed* to forget. She swallowed. Like the night of the ball when she'd let her raging hormones get the better of her and had ended up on the bed with him. When passion and anger had fused in an explosive sexual cocktail and, for a short and surreal period, she had found herself yearning for the impossible.

And now?

She turned away from the window, where the palace gardens looked like a blurred kaleidoscope before her unseeing eyes.

Now she felt nothing but a deep sense of sadness as she met his piercing sapphire gaze.

'What is there left to say?' she questioned

tiredly. 'I thought we'd said it all on the night of the ball. Considering what happened, I thought we'd adapted to a bad situation rather well.'

'You think so?' His eyebrows arched. 'With me occupying my former bachelor apartments while you sleep alone in the marital suite?'

'What's the matter, Luc? It can't be the sex you're missing. I mean, it isn't as if we were at it like rabbits before all this blew up, is it?'

'There's no need to be crude,' he snapped.

If they'd been a normal couple Lisa might have made a wry joke about that remark, but they weren't. They were about as far from normal as you could get—two strangers living in a huge palace which somehow felt as claustrophobic as if they were stuck in some tenement apartment.

'Are you worried what people are saying?' she demanded. 'Is that it? Afraid the servants will gossip about the Prince and Princess leading separate lives?' She pushed a handful of curls away from her hot face and fixed him with a steady look. 'Don't you think that's something they should get used to?'

Luc clenched the fists which were stuffed deep in the pockets of his trousers and tried very hard not to react to his wife's angry taunts. If he'd been worried about gossip he would never have brought her back here. He would never have... He closed his eyes in a moment of frustration. How far back did he have to go to think about all the things he *wouldn't* do with her—and why couldn't he shake off the feeling that somehow all his good intentions were meaningless, because he felt *powerless* when it came to Lisa?

He shook his head. 'No. I'm not worried about what people are saying.'

'Maybe you're still regretting the other night?' she said softly. 'Wishing you hadn't had sex with me?'

Luc swallowed as her words conjured up a series of mental images he'd tried to keep off limits but now they hurtled into his mind in vivid and disturbing technicolour. Lisa pushing him back onto the bed. Lisa on top of him in the billowing crimson dress, her face flushed with passion as she rode him. His mouth dried. He *wanted* to regret what had happened, but how could he when it had been one of the most erotic encounters of his life? He had felt like her puppet. Her slave. And hadn't that turned him on even more? Dazed and confused, he had left their suite afterwards and stumbled to the library to discover that what she'd said had been true—that pregnant women *did* have sex. It seemed his wife had been right and there were some things he *didn't* know about women.

Especially about her.

'No, I'm not regretting that.'

'What, then?'

His gaze bored into her. 'Why didn't you tell me that Eleonora persuaded you to wear the necklace?'

'Why bother shooting the messenger?' she answered. 'Eleonora might have had her own agenda but she wasn't the one who made you react like that. You did that all by yourself.' She glanced at him from between her lashes. 'Did she tell you?'

'No,' he said grimly. 'I overheard her saying something about it to one of the other aides and asked to see her.'

'Gosh. That must have been a fun discussion,' she said flippantly. 'Did she persuade you that it had been a perfectly innocent gesture on her part? Flutter those big eyes at you and tell you that you'd be better off with her beloved Princess Sophie?'

'I wasn't in the mood for any kind of *explanation*,' he bit out angrily. 'And neither was I in the mood for her hysterical response when I sacked her.'

Lisa blinked. 'You...*sacked* her?'

'Of course I did.' He fixed her with a cool stare. 'Do you really think I would tolerate that kind of subversive attitude in my palace? Or have an aide actively trying to make trouble for my wife?'

Lisa didn't know what to think. She'd been stupid and gullible in agreeing to Eleonora's suggestion that she 'surprise' Luc, but she shouldn't allow herself to forget why she had embraced the idea so eagerly in the first place. She had wanted to impress him. To show him she was willing to be a good wife and a good princess. And if she was being brutally honest—hadn't she been secretly longing for some kind of answering epiphany in him? Hoping that the emotional tide might be about to turn with her first public presentation?

But it hadn't and it never would. If anything, the situation was a million times worse. The sex had awoken her sleeping senses but highlighted the great gulf which lay between them. And wouldn't she be the world's biggest fool if she started demanding something from a man who was incapable of delivering it?

She stared at him. 'So what do you want to talk about?'

Repressing another frustrated sigh, Luc met her gaze, knowing there was no such thing as an easy solution. But had he expected any different? She was the most complicated and frustrating woman he'd ever met. He gave a bitter smile. And never had he wanted anyone more.

When she had walked towards him at the Mardovian Embassy in her subdued wedding finery, he had made a silent vow to be the best husband and father he possibly could be, and he had meant it. Yet now he could see that it might have been a challenge too far. *Because he didn't know how to be those things.* And for a woman who was naturally suspicious of men— He suspected that he and Lisa were the worst possible combination.

So did he have the strength to do what he needed to do? To set her free from her palace prison? To release her from a relationship which had been doomed from the start? It wasn't a question of choice, he realised—but one of necessity. He had to do it. A lump rose in his throat. He could do it for her.

'Do you want to go back to England?' he questioned quietly. 'Not straight away, of course. But once the baby is born.'

Lisa jerked back her head and looked at him with suspicious eyes. 'You mean you'll let me go?'

'Yes, Lisa.' He gave a mocking smile. 'I'll release you from your prison.'

'And you're prepared to discuss shared custody?' Now she was blinking her eyes very hard. 'That's very…civilised of you, Luc.'

His mouth twisted. 'None of this sounds remotely civilised to me—but it's clearly what you want. And I am not so much of a tyrant to keep you here against your will.'

She lifted her clear gaze to him. 'Thank you,' she said.

He walked away from her, increasing the distance between them, removing himself from the tantalising danger of her proximity. But once he had reached the imposing marble fireplace, he halted, his face grave. 'I guess we should look on the bright side. At least now we've had sex, it means that our marriage has been legitimised and our child will be born as the true heir to Mardovia.'

She stiffened, her lips parting as she stared at him. '*What* did you say?'

'I was just stating facts,' he answered coolly. 'Up until the other night our marriage wasn't legal because we hadn't consummated it.'

'Was that why you did it? Why you let me make love to you?' she whispered, her face blanching. 'Just to make our marriage *legal*?'

'Please don't insult me, Lisa. We both know why I had sex with you that night and it had nothing to do with legality.' He met her gaze for a long moment before turning away from her. 'And now, if you'll excuse me—I have a meeting with my ministers, which I really can't delay any longer.'

Lisa watched him go but it wasn't until he had closed the door behind him that she collapsed on the nearest chair as the significance of his words began to sink in. He was letting her go. After the baby was born, he was going to let her leave the island. She would no longer be forced to stay in this farce of a marriage with a cold man who could only ever express himself in bed. He would probably give her a house, just as he had given one to her sister, and she would be free to live her life on *her* terms.

So why did she feel as if someone had twisted her up in tight knots?

She forced herself to be logical. To think with her head instead of her heart. As Luc's estranged wife, she would never again have financial worries. And she would work hard at forging an amicable relationship with Luc. That would be a priority. They wouldn't become one of those bitter divorced couples who made their child's life a misery by their constant warring.

But Lisa couldn't shake off her sudden sense of emptiness as she went to her studio and looked at her sketches she'd been making for her next collection. Maybe she should make some more. Because what else was she going to do during the days leading up to the birth? Prowl around the palace like a bulky shadow, staring at all the beauty and storing it away in her memory to pull out on lonely days back in England—as if to remind herself that this hadn't all been some surreal dream.

For the next few days she immersed herself completely in her work. She began drawing with a sudden intensity—her designs taking on clean new lines as she liaised with her workshop back in London about an overall vision for the new collection. She worked long sessions from dawn to dusk—punctuated only by brisk walks in the gardens, where sometimes she would sit on a stone bench and watch the sunlight cast glittering patterns on the sapphire sea far below—and tried not to wonder what her husband was doing.

Mostly he left her alone, but one evening he came to her studio, walking in after a brief knock, to find her bent over a swatch of fabrics.

'Don't you think you're overdoing the work ethic a little?' he observed, with a frown. 'One of the servants told me you've been here since sunrise.'

'I couldn't sleep. And I'm nearly finished. I just want to get this last bit done.'

'You're looking tired,' he said critically. 'You need to rest.'

But this single concerned intervention had been the exception, because mostly she only saw him at mealtimes. Perhaps he was already withdrawing from her and preparing for the reality of their separation. And in truth, it was better this way. She spent a lot of time convincing herself of that. It was how it was going to be and she had better get used to it.

Dr Gautier visited daily, pronouncing himself quietly satisfied at her progress—and if he wondered why Luc no longer attended any of the appointments, he made no mention of it. That was yet another of the advantages of being royal, Lisa realised. People just accepted what you did and never dared challenge you—and that couldn't be a good thing. It would make you grow up thinking that you could fashion the world according to whim. Wasn't that what Luc had done by bringing her here and forcing her to marry him?

She was over a week away from her due date when the first pain came in the middle of the night, waking her up with a start. A ring of steel clamped itself around her suddenly rock-hard belly and Lisa clutched her arms around it in the darkness, trying to remember the midwife's instructions. It was the early hours of the morning and the contractions were very irregular—she had plenty of time before she needed to let anyone know.

But as they got stronger and more painful, she rang for Almeera, whose eyes widened when she saw her mistress sitting on the edge of the bed, rocking forward and back.

'Fetch the Prince,' said Lisa, closing her eyes as she felt the onset of another fierce contraction. 'Tell him I'm in labour.'

Luc arrived almost immediately, looking as if he'd just thrown his clothes on and not bothered to tidy his hair. His cell phone was pressed to his ear as he walked into the room, his gaze raking over her.

'Dr Gautier wants to know how often the contractions are coming,' he said.

'Every…' She gasped as she glanced at the golden clock on the mantelpiece. 'Every five minutes.'

He relayed this information, slipping naturally into French before cutting the connection. 'The ambulance is on its way and so is Dr Gautier.'

She gazed up at him. 'My…my waters have broken,' she stumbled.

He smiled. 'Well, that is normal, isn't it, *chérie*?'

His soft tone disarmed her and so did his confidence. It made her forget about the distance between them. And suddenly Lisa wanted more than his support—she needed some of his strength. And comfort. 'Luc?' she said brokenly as another contraction came—surely far sooner than it was supposed to.

He was by her side in an instant, taking her hand and not flinching when her fingernails bit into his flesh as another contraction powered over her. 'I'm here,' he said.

'I'm supposed to have the baby in the hospital,' she whispered.

'It doesn't matter where you have the baby,' he said. 'We have everything here you need. You're going to be fine.'

And somehow she believed him, even when Dr Gautier arrived with another doctor and two midwives and said there was no time to go anywhere. All the things she'd read about were starting to happen, only now they were happening to *her*. At first she was scared and then it all became too intense to be anything but focussed. She tried to concentrate on her breathing, aware of the immense pressure building up inside her and Luc smoothing back her sweat-tangled curls. The medical staff were speaking to each other very quickly—sometimes in French—but Luc was murmuring to her in English. Telling her that she was brave and strong. Telling her that she could do this. She could do anything.

And then it was happening. The urge to push and being told she couldn't push, and then being unable to do anything *but* push. Still gripping Luc's hand, Lisa gritted her teeth and tried to pant the way she'd been taught—and just as she thought the contractions couldn't get any more intense, her baby was delivered into the hands of the waiting doctor and a loud and penetrating wail filled the air.

'*C'est une fille!*' exclaimed Dr Gautier.

'A girl?' said Lisa, looking up into Luc's eyes.

He nodded. 'A beautiful baby girl,' he said unsteadily, his eyes suddenly very bright.

Lisa slumped back against the pillows as a sense of quiet and purposeful activity took over. The intensity of the birth had morphed into an air of serenity as the doctor finished his examinations, and, now cocooned in soft white cashmere, the baby was handed to her.

She felt so light, thought Lisa as a shaft of something fierce and protective shot through her. So light and yet so strong. With unfamiliar fingers, she guided her daughter to her breast, where she immediately began to suckle. Dimly, she became aware that Luc had left the room and, once the baby had finished feeding, the midwives helped her wash and gave her a clean silk nightgown. And when she next looked up, Luc was back and it was just the three of them.

She felt strangely shy as he dragged up a gilt chair and sat beside her, his elbows on his knees, his palms cupping his chin as he watched her intently. Their eyes met over the baby's head and Lisa suddenly felt a powerful sense of longing, wishing he would reach out and touch her. But they didn't have that kind of relationship, she reminded herself. They'd gone too far in the wrong direction and there was no turning back.

'We need to discuss names,' she said.

'Names?' he echoed blankly.

'We can't keep calling her "the baby". Are you still happy with Rose and then both our mothers' names?'

'Rose Maria Elizabeth,' he said, his slow gaze taking in every centimetre of the baby's face. 'They are perfect. Just like her.'

'Rose,' Lisa echoed softly, before holding out the snowy bundle towards him. 'Would you like to hold her?'

Luc's hesitation was brief as he reached out but his heart maintained its powerful pounding as he held his baby for the first time. He had never known real fear before, but he knew it now. Fear that he would prove inadequate to care for this tiny bundle of humanity. Fear that he might say the wrong thing to the woman who had just blown him away by giving birth to her.

As he cradled his sleeping daughter and marvelled at her sheer tininess, he felt the thick layer of ice around his heart begin to fracture. He could feel the welling up of unknown emotion—a whole great storm of it—packed down so deeply inside him that he hadn't even realised it was there. It felt raw and it felt painful, but it felt *real*—this sudden rush of devotion and a determination to protect his child for as long as he lived.

'Thank you,' he said softly, glancing up to meet Lisa's eyes.

'You're welcome.'

He saw the cloud which crossed like a shadow over her beautiful face but there was no need to ask what had caused it. For although their child had been born safely and mother and daughter were healthy, none of their other problems had gone away. They were still estranged. Still leading separate lives, with Lisa no doubt counting down the days until she could return to England. Concentrating only on her shadowed eyes, he stood up, carrying Rose over to her crib and laying her gently down before looking at Lisa's pinched face.

'You're exhausted,' he said. 'Shall I phone your sister and tell her the news and you can speak to her yourself later?'

She folded her lips together as if she didn't trust herself to speak, and nodded.

Resisting the desire to go over and drop a grateful kiss onto her beautiful lips, he took one last look at her before walking over to the door. 'Go to sleep now, Lisa,' he said unevenly. 'Just go to sleep.'

CHAPTER ELEVEN

IT WAS LIKE living in a bubble.

A shining golden bubble.

Lisa woke up every morning feeling as if she weren't part of the outside world any more. As if her experience was nothing like that of other women in her situation—and she supposed that much was true. Most new mothers didn't live in a beautiful palace with servants falling over themselves to make her life easier. And most new mothers didn't have a husband who was barely able to look at them without a dark and sombre expression on his face.

She told herself to be grateful that Luc clearly adored their daughter, and she was. It made a lump stick in her throat to see how gentle he was with their baby. It was humbling to see such a powerful man being reduced to putty by the starfish hands of his daughter, which would curl themselves tightly around his fingers as she gazed up at him with blue eyes so like his own.

Lisa would sit watching him play with Rose, but the calm expression she wore didn't reflect the turmoil she was feeling inside. Did Luc feel just as conflicted? she wondered. She didn't know because they didn't talk about it. They discussed the fact that their daughter had the bluest eyes in the world and the sweetest nature, but *they didn't talk about anything which mattered.*

Before the birth he'd promised Lisa she could return to England, and she knew she had to broach the subject some time. But something was stopping her and that something was the voice of her conscience. She had started to wonder how she could possibly take Rose away from here, denying Luc the daily parenting he so clearly enjoyed.

Because Lisa had never had that kind of hands-on fathering. When her own father had died she'd been too young to remember if he cuddled her or read her stories at night. And she'd never really had the chance to ask her mother because she had remarried so quickly. All evidence of the man who had died had been ruthlessly eradicated from the house. Her new stepfather had been so intolerant of her and Brittany that the two little girls had walked around on eggshells, terrified of stirring up a rage which had never been far from the surface. They'd learnt never to speak unless spoken to and they'd learnt never to demand any of their mother's time. Lisa had watched helplessly as he had whittled away at their fortune—

and she wondered if it had been that which had made her so fiercely independent. Was the lack of love in their childhood the reason why Brittany had jettisoned her university course and fallen straight into the arms of the first man to show her some affection?

All Lisa knew was that she couldn't contemplate bringing Rose up without love. At the moment things were tolerable because it was all so new. She was getting used to motherhood and Luc was getting used to fatherhood. But the atmosphere between the two of them was at best polite. They were like two people stuck together in a broken-down lift, saying only as much as they needed to—but it wouldn't stay like that, would it? Once they were out of the baby-shock phase, things would return to 'normal'. But she and Luc had no 'normal'. Sooner or later they were going to start wanting different things.

She decided to speak to him about it after dinner one evening—a meal they still took together, mainly, she suspected, to maintain some sort of charade in front of the staff.

Leaving Almeera with Rose, Lisa washed her hair before slipping into a long, silk tunic which disguised the extra heaviness of her breasts and tummy. She even put on a little make-up, wondering why she was going to so much trouble. *Because I want to look in control.* I want to show him that I mean business.

But when she popped her head in to check on Rose before going down for dinner, it was to find Luc standing by the crib, his fingers touching the baby's soft black hair as he murmured to her softly.

'Oh,' she said. 'You're here.'

He glanced over at Almeera, who was fiddling with the intricate mobile which hung over the crib. 'I wonder if you'd mind leaving us for a moment, Almeera,' he said.

The servant nodded and slipped away and Lisa looked at Luc, feeling suddenly disorientated.

'I thought we were having dinner,' she said.

He raised his eyebrows. 'I think we're able to apply a little flexibility about the time we eat, don't you?' he said drily. 'Unless you're especially hungry.'

Lisa shrugged, wondering why tonight he was looking at her more intently than he had done for weeks. Automatically, she skated a palm down over the curve of one hip without considering the wisdom of such an action. 'I ought to be cutting back on food,' she said.

'Don't be ridiculous,' he said, his voice growing a little impatient before it gentled. 'You look beautiful, if you really want to know. Luscious and ripe and womanly.'

Actually, she didn't want to know and she didn't want his voice dipping into a sensual caress like that, making her long for something which

definitely *wasn't* on the menu. She took an unsteady breath. 'We have to discuss the future,'
she said.

There was a pause. 'I know we do.'

Luc looked into the questioning face of his wife
and wondered afterwards if it was the sense of a
looming ultimatum and dread which made him
drop his guard so completely. He stared at her
shiny hazelnut curls and the fleshy curves of her
body and he felt his throat dry to dust as he forced
himself to confront the truth.

Because in a sudden flash of insight he realised that the feelings he had were not just for
their child, but for the woman who had given birth
to her. A woman he'd brought here as a hostage,
but who had tried to reach out to him all the same.
He could recognise it now but he'd been too blind
to see at the time. Because once her initial opposition to being his wife had faded, he realised that
she'd tried to make the best of her life here. She
had studied the history of his country and quietly
gone about her own career without making undue
demands on his time.

But despite the silent vow he'd made on their
wedding day, he had continued to keep her at arm's
length, hadn't he? He had kept himself at a physical distance even though he'd sensed that she'd
wanted him. He had deliberately not laid a finger
on her, knowing that such a move was calculated

to make her desire for him grow. To *frustrate* her. And deep down, his disapproval had never been far from the surface. If he was being honest, hadn't he experienced a certain *relief* that he'd been able to chastise her over the damned necklace? As if he had needed something to justify why he could never allow himself to get close to her. The truth was that he had treated Lisa as an object rather than a person. *Because he hadn't known how to do it any other way.*

But suddenly he did—or at least, he thought he did. Was Rose responsible for opening the flood-gates? Emotion flooded over him like a warm tide as he looked down at his daughter. Tentatively, she opened her eyes, and as he gazed into a sapphire hue so like his own he felt his heart clench. He lifted his head to meet Lisa's watchful gaze, the dryness in his throat making the thought of speech seem impossible, but that was no excuse. Because this was something he could not turn away from. Something he could no longer deny.

'I love her, Lisa,' he said simply.

For a moment there was silence before she nodded. 'I know. Me, too. It's funny, isn't it?' She gave a little laugh, as if she was embarrassed to hear him say the words out loud. 'How you can feel it so instantly and completely.'

Luc drew in a deep breath as he met her eyes. He thought about the first time he'd met her and that rare glint of shared understanding which had passed between them. The way he hadn't been able to get her out of his head in all the months which had followed. When he'd seen her again, the chemistry between them was as explosive as it had ever been—but what he felt now was about more than sex. Much more. Because somehow he'd come to realise that his spunky designer with the clear green-gold gaze treated him as nobody else had ever done.

She treated him like a man and not a prince.

So tell her. Take courage and tell her the words you never imagined you'd say.

'And I love you, too, Lisa,' he said. 'More than I'd ever realised.'

At first Lisa thought she must be dreaming, because surely Luc hadn't just told her that he loved her? She blinked. But he had. Even if the words hadn't still been resonating on the air, she knew she hadn't misheard them from the look on his face, which seemed to be savage yet silky, all at the same time. She felt a shiver whispering its way over her skin as she tried to ignore the sensual softening of his lips and to concentrate on facts, not dreams. Be careful what you wish for—that was what people said, wasn't it? And suddenly she understood why.

Luc had let his cold mask slip for a moment. Or rather, it hadn't *slipped*—he had just replaced it with a different mask. A loving mask which was far more suitable for ensuring he got what he wanted.

His baby.

Yet she wouldn't have been human if her first response hadn't been a fierce burst of hope. If she hadn't pictured the tumultuous scene which could follow, if she let it. Of her nodding her head and letting all the tears which were gathering force spill from her eyes before telling him shakily that yes, she loved him, too.

And, oh, the exquisite irony of that—even if it happened to be true. Admitting she loved a man who was cold-bloodedly trying to manipulate her emotions by saying something he didn't mean. What about all the lessons she was supposed to have learnt?

He was looking at her from between narrowed lashes and she knew she had to strike now. Before she had the chance to change her mind and cling to him and beg him to never let her go.

'Do you think I'm stupid?' she questioned quietly, her voice low and unsteady. 'Because I would have to be pretty stupid not to realise why you just told me you loved me. You don't *love* me, Luc. You've fallen in love with your daughter, yes— and I'm over the moon about that. But this isn't like going to the supermarket—which you've probably never done. We don't come as a two-for-one deal! And you can't smooth-talk me into staying on Mardovia just because you've trotted out the conditional emotional clause which most women are brainless enough to fall for!'

He went very still, his powerful body seeming to become the whole dark focus of the room. 'You think I told you I loved you because I have an ulterior motive?' he questioned slowly.

'I don't think it—I *know* it!'

He flinched and nodded his head. 'I had no idea you thought quite so badly of me, Lisa.'

Something in the quiet dignity of his words made Lisa's heart contract with pain, but she couldn't retract her accusation now—and why should she? He was trying to manipulate her in every which way and she wouldn't let him. She couldn't *afford* to let him. Because she'd crumble if he hurt her, and she never crumbled.

'I don't think badly of you,' she said. 'I think you're a great dad and that's what's making you say all this stuff. But you don't have to pretend in order to make things work. I want things to be… amicable between us, Luc.'

'Amicable?' he bit out before slowly nodding his head, and in that moment Lisa saw a cold acceptance settle over his features. 'Very well. If that's what you want, then that's what you'll get.' There was a pause. 'When *exactly* do you want to leave?'

Lisa and Rose's journey was scheduled for the end of the week. She was to fly back to London with Rose and Almeera and two protection officers, who would move into a section of Luc's large London house, which would now be her home. The idea of two of Luc's henchmen spying on her filled her with dread and Lisa tried to assert her independence.

'I don't need two protection officers,' she told Luc.

'You may not, but my daughter does.'

Lisa licked her lips. 'So I'm trapped any which way?'

He shrugged. 'Trapped or protected—it all depends how you look at it. And now, if you've quite finished, there are things I'd like to do while Rose is still in residence, and today I'd like to take her into Vallemar to meet some friends.'

Lisa told herself she didn't want to be parted from her baby and that was why she asked the question. 'Can't I come?'

'Why?' he questioned coolly. 'These are people you are unlikely to see in the future—so why bother getting to know them? No point in complicating an already complicated situation.'

So Lisa was forced to watch as Luc, Rose and

Almeera were driven away in one of the palace limousines while she stayed put. She paced the gardens, unable to settle until they returned— with an exquisite selection of tiny Parisian couture dresses for Rose, from someone called Michele— and Lisa could do nothing about the sudden jealous pounding of her heart. But she didn't dare ask Luc who Michele was. Even she could recognise that she didn't have the right to do that.

At last, after a final sleepless night, it was time to leave. Lisa stood awkwardly in the main entrance of the palace, feeling small and very isolated as she prepared to say goodbye to Luc. Already in the car with Almeera, Rose was buckled into her baby seat—but now there was nothing but a terrible sense of impending doom as Lisa looked up into the stony features of her royal husband.

'Well,' she said, her bright voice sounding cracked. 'I guess this is it. And you'll…you'll be over to London next week?'

'I'll be over whenever I damned well please and I shall come and go as I please,' he said, his blue eyes glittering out a warning. 'So don't think you can move some freeloader into my house while I'm away, because I will not tolerate it.'

Don't rise to it, thought Lisa. Don't leave with the memory of angry words between you. She nodded instead. 'I have no intention of doing that, which I suspect you already know. So…goodbye, Luc. I'll… I'll be seeing you.'

And suddenly his cold mask seemed to dissolve to reveal the etching of anger and pain which lay behind. Did he realise she had witnessed it? Was that why he reached out and gripped her arms, his fingers pressing into the soft flesh, as if wanting to reassert the control he had momentarily lost?

'Better have something other than a tame good-bye to remember me by, dear wife,' he said. 'Don't you agree?'

And before she could raise any objection, his lips were pressing down on hers in a punishing kiss which was all about possession and nothing whatsoever to do with affection. But it worked. Oh, how quickly it worked. It had her opening her lips beneath the seeking pressure of his and gasping softly as she felt the tip of his tongue sliding over hers. She swayed slightly and as his big hands steadied her she could feel the clamour of her suddenly hungry body as it demanded more. Touch me, she thought silently, wishing that they were somewhere less public, though pretty sure none of the servants were around. Just *touch* me.

But just as suddenly he terminated the kiss— stepping away from her, the triumph darkening his eyes not quite managing to hide his contempt, so that she could hardly bear to look at him. As she stumbled out of the door towards the car she could feel his gaze burning into her back.

Rose was sleeping and Almeera was sitting in the front beside the driver as the car headed towards the airfield, and all Lisa could think about was Luc. Raw pain ripped through her. She found herself wishing that it could all have been different. Wishing he'd meant it when he told her that he loved her.

They were almost at the airfield when her thoughts jarred and then jammed—the way CDs used to get stuck if there was a fault on the disc and started repeating the same piece of music over and over again. She creased her brow as she tried to work out what it was which was bothering her.

She found herself remembering what he'd told her about his upbringing and the women paid to look after him after his mother's death. His words had moved her, despite the flat and matter-of-fact way in which he'd delivered them—as if he were reading from the minutes of a boring meeting. But you would have needed a heart of stone not to be affected by the thought of the lonely little boy growing up alone in a palace, with nobody but a grieving father and a series of strict governesses for company.

Had those governesses ever told him they loved him? Held him tightly in their arms and hugged him and kissed his little head? She bit her lip. Of course not—because that hadn't been in their job description. They had been there to serve. To drum in his duty to his country. A duty he must be reminded of whenever he saw the Wheeler portraits of Louisa De Lacy, whose love affair with his ancestor had almost destroyed the Mardovian dynasty. But it had not. The principality had survived and today it was strong—and powerful.

Yet despite all his wealth and power, Luc had not fought her for his daughter's custody, had he? With his access to the world's finest lawyers she sensed he had the ability to do that—and to win— so why hadn't he?

What did that say about him as a man? That he could be understanding, yes. Magnanimous, compassionate and kind. Or even that he cared more about her happiness and Rose's than about his own.

That he *loved* her?

She stared out of the car window and thought about how closed up he could seem. About the courage it must have taken for him to come out and say something like that. The way his voice had cracked with emotion as he'd spoken—and she knew then that he would never have said it if he didn't mean it. He had even told her that, once. Yet she had just batted his words back to him as if they'd been of no consequence, hadn't she? She had turned away from him, too frightened and so entrenched in her own prejudices to believe him.

For how could either of them know about the giving and receiving of love if neither of them had ever witnessed it?

'Stop the car!' she yelled, before recovering herself slightly and leaning forward to speak to the driver. 'Please. Can you take us back to the palace?'

Lisa's heart was racing during a drive back which seemed to take much longer than the outward journey, and she couldn't stop thinking that maybe it was already too late. What if he'd gone out, or refused to see her, or…?

But there were a million variations on 'what if' and she tried to push them from her mind as they drove up the mountain road with the beautiful blue bay glittering far below.

Leaving Almeera to bring Rose inside, Lisa went rushing into the palace, knowing that she should be walking calmly in a manner befitting a princess—even if she was an estranged one—but she couldn't seem to stop herself. She was about to ask one of the footmen where she could find the Prince when she saw Luc's rather terrifying new aide, Serge, coming from the direction of one of the smaller anterooms.

'I need to see the Prince,' she blurted out.

Serge's face remained impassive. 'The Prince

has left strict instructions that under no circumstances is he to be disturbed.'

Had her departure already robbed her of any small vestige of power her royal status might once have given her? Stubbornly, Lisa shook her head and sped noiselessly in the direction she'd seen Serge walking from.

With shaking fingers she opened doors. The first room was empty, as was the second, but in the third Luc stood alone by the window, his body tense and his shoulders hunched as he stared out.

Behind her Lisa could hear rapid footsteps and she turned round to see that the Russian had almost caught her up.

'Your Highness…' Serge began.

'Leave us, Serge,' said Luc, without turning round.

Lisa's heart was pounding but she waited until the aide had retreated and closed the door behind him before she risked saying anything.

'Luc,' she said breathlessly, but all the things she'd been meaning to say just died in her throat as nerves overcame her.

He turned around then, very slowly, and she was shocked by the ravaged expression on his face— at the deep sense of sorrow which seemed to envelop him, like a dark cloud. His sapphire eyes were icy-cold and she'd never seen someone look quite so unwelcoming.

'Where's Rose?' he demanded.

'Almeera's just bringing her in. I needed...' she swallowed '...to speak to you.'

'Haven't we said everything which needs to be said, Lisa? Haven't we completely exhausted the subject?'

'No,' she said, knowing that she needed the courage to reach into her frightened heart, despite the forbidding look on his face. 'We haven't.'

But clearly he wasn't about to help her. 'What do you want?' he questioned impatiently, as if she were a servant who had neglected to remove one of the plates.

'I want to tell you,' she whispered, before drawing in a deep breath, 'how very stupid I've been. And to try to tell you why.'

'I'm not interested in your explanations,' he snapped.

'I want to explain,' she continued, with a sudden feeling of calm and certainty, which she sensed was her only lifeline, 'that I was scared when you told me you loved me. Scared you didn't mean it. Scared I'd get hurt—'

'And you've spent your whole life avoiding getting hurt, haven't you, Lisa?' he finished slowly, as if he had just worked it out for himself. 'You learnt a bitter lesson at your mother's knee that love could destroy you.'

'Yes. *Yes!* Those feelings aren't always logical, but that doesn't make them any less valid. That's why I finished with you the first time.' She stared down at her shiny gold wedding band, before lifting her gaze to his. 'Oh, I knew there was no future in it—you told me that right from the start—but that wasn't why. Because who wouldn't have wanted to prolong every wonderful second of what we had? It was because I had started to fall in love with you and I knew that was a mistake. You didn't want love. Not from me. You told me you didn't want anything from me. I tried to forget you—I tried so very hard—and then when you walked into the shop that day, I realised nothing had changed.' She shrugged. 'Not a single thing. I still wanted you.'

'And I still wanted you,' he said. 'Even though everything about it was wrong and even though I tried to resist you, in the end I couldn't.'

'Maybe you just can't resist sex when it's offered to you on a plate.'

'Oh, but I can,' he assured her softly. 'I hadn't— haven't—had sex with anyone else since my relationship with you first ended.'

She stared at him in disbelief. 'Nobody?'

'Nobody.'

'But why? I mean, why not? There must have been plenty of opportunities to bed all kinds of women.'

Luc rubbed his thumb over his lips, realising

that you could say words of love and mean them, but that was only the beginning. Because you needed to go deeper than that. To be prepared to show another person every part of you—to draw aside the curtain of mystique and admit that inside even *he* could be vulnerable.

'Initially I convinced myself that I needed a time of celibacy before settling down with Sophie, but that wasn't the real reason.' He shook his head and shrugged. 'Because the truth was that I just didn't want anyone else but you, Lisa. I don't know how and I don't know why—but you're the woman who has made me feel stuff I didn't even realise existed. The only one. And I want—'

'No,' she rushed in, as if eager to show him her own vulnerability. 'Let me tell you what I want, Luc. I want to be a real wife to you, in every sense of the word. I want to live here or anywhere, just so long as it's with you and Rose. I'd like to have more children, if you would. And I'd like to be the best princess I can possibly be. I want time to love you and to show you all the stuff I've never dared show you before. So what have you got to say to that, Luciano Gabriel Leonidas? Will you take me on?'

He could feel the powerful beat of his heart as he pulled her into his arms, but for the first time in his adult life he realised that his cheeks were wet with tears. And so were hers. He dried them with his lips and then bent his head so his mouth met hers. 'I'll take you on any time you like,' he said unsteadily, just before he kissed her. 'Because I love you.'

EPILOGUE

'IS SHE ASLEEP?'

'Flat out.' Lisa walked into their bedroom, pulling the elastic band from her hair and letting her curls tumble free. Luc was lying on top of the bed, reading. His eyes slitted as he watched her and he put the book down and smiled.

Lisa smiled back as her heart gave an unsteady thunder as she looked at her beloved husband. The light from the sunset was bathing everything in rose gold as it flooded in through the open windows—turning his naked body into a gilded statue. He really was magnificent, she thought hungrily, enjoying the way that the glowing light highlighted the hard muscle and silken flesh of his physique. She looked into his eyes, thinking how very quickly time passed and how important it was to treasure every single moment.

Sometimes it was hard to believe that their daughter was already two years old and probably the most sophisticated little jet-setter of all her peers. But everyone said that Princess Rose had the sweetest and sunniest nature in the world and her besotted parents tended to agree with them.

She wiped her still-damp hands down over her dress. 'Your daughter seems to think that bath time was made for fun,' she observed, with a smile.

'Just like her mother.' Luc's eyes gleamed. 'I think you and I might share a shower in a little while, but I have other plans for you first.'

'Oh? What plans?'

'Well, you are looking a little overdressed compared to me.' A lazy gesture of his hand lingered fractionally over his hardening body and he slanted her a complicit smile. 'So why don't you take off your dress and come over here?'

'That sounds like a very sensible idea to me,' she murmured, shivering a little with anticipation as she pulled the dress over her head and joined him on the bed.

He unclipped the rose-black lace of her bra and bent his mouth to the puckered point of her nipple, giving it a luxurious lick, before raising his eyes to hers. 'Looking forward to tomorrow?'

'I can't wait.'

He smiled. 'Then I guess we'd better do something to help pass the time as satisfactorily as possible. Don't you?'

Lisa stroked her toes against his foot as he

slithered her panties down. Tomorrow the three of them were joining Brittany, Jason and Tamsin for a week-long break on the quieter southwestern shores of Mardovia—a sprawling idyll of a royal retreat, well away from all the servants and protocol of the main palace. It was one of the few places where they could be totally free, but Lisa accepted that the occasional loss of freedom was the price to be paid for the honour of ruling this ancient island alongside her husband. And she was happy to pay it, because she had worked hard to ensure her smooth transition into palace life and all its expectations.

Early on she'd recognised that maintaining a business in England while trying to settle into her new role was probably not sustainable in the long term—though Luc had told her that if she wanted to continue, then somehow they would make it happen. But being a full-time designer did not fit in with being a full-time princess and mother— and a part-time designer was never going to make waves. So she sold the label and the few pangs of regret she experienced soon passed.

Luc had invested in and commandeered the building of a new Art and Fashion School, which was named after her, and she had been taken aback and humbled by this gesture of his love. She was proud and honoured to be the patron of the state-of-the-art institution and planned to give monthly lectures on design, as well as making sure Mardovia became a hub for fashion innovation. There was a lot of young talent on this island, she realised—and she was going to make sure that every Mardovian child's talent would be fulfilled.

She had tried very hard to understand Eleonora's behaviour towards her. Lisa soon recognised that it had been an overdeveloped sense of patriotism and rather warped sense of devotion towards Luc which had made the aide resent the new commoner princess so much. But, as Lisa whispered to Luc one evening, she didn't want to start out her royal life with enemies, and forgiveness was good for the soul. So she had given Eleonora a key administrative role in the new Art School, and Eleonora had rewarded her with genuine loyalty ever since.

She and Luc had done everything in the wrong order, Lisa reflected ruefully as her panties fluttered to the floor. Her pregnancy had come before the wedding and there hadn't been a honeymoon for many months—not until Rose had been settled enough to leave with Almeera.

The other big change was with Jason. Brittany's new-found independence had given her the strength to tell Jason that there was no future for them until he got himself a job. And she'd meant it. Jason had found himself a job in a warehouse and had put in the hours and the backbone. It wasn't the most glamorous job in the world, but it proved something to them all—that Tamsin's father did have grit and commitment somewhere inside him. Six months later he and Britt were married and Luc offered him a role with his security facility at the Mardovian Embassy in London.

'What are you smiling to yourself for?' Luc's deep voice interrupted her reverie—as did the finger drifting over her ribcage—and Lisa looked into the sapphire gleam of her husband's eyes.

'I'm just thinking how perfect my life is.'

'I'm pleased to hear it. Perhaps I can think of a way to make it even more perfect.'

She batted her eyelashes. 'Really?'

'Really.' A smoky look entered his eyes as he brushed his lips over hers. 'I intend making love to you until the moon is high in the sky, *chérie*— but first there is something I need to do.'

She lifted her hand to his face, resting it tenderly against the angled contours of his cheek. 'Which is?' she whispered, though she knew what was coming for it was something of a daily ritual for them—a glorious reaffirming of the vows they had once made under duress. At times they had each felt this particular emotion, but neither of them had dared say it, but now the words could be spoken freely and spoken from the heart. And they said them just as often as they could, as if to remind themselves of their good fortune.

'I love you,' he said softly.

Was it crazy that tears had begun to prick at the backs of her eyes? Lisa didn't care because she no longer shied away from showing emotion. And when something felt this good, you just had to let it all come rushing out.

'I love you, too, my darling Luc,' she whispered back. 'Now and for ever.'

And she drew his dark head towards her so that she could kiss him, in a room gilded rose gold by the glorious Mardovian sunset.

* * * * *

If you enjoyed this story,
check out these other great reads
from Sharon Kendrick
THE BILLIONAIRE'S DEFIANT ACQUISITION
THE SHEIKH'S CHRISTMAS CONQUEST
CLAIMED FOR MAKAROV'S BABY
THE RUTHLESS GREEK'S RETURN
Available now!

Coming soon to the
ONE NIGHT WITH CONSEQUENCES *series*
THE SHEIKH'S BABY SCANDAL
by Carol Marinelli
Available September 2016

COMING NEXT MONTH FROM

◆ HARLEQUIN

Presents®

Available August 23, 2016

#3457 TO BLACKMAIL A DI SIONE
The Billionaire's Legacy
by Rachael Thomas

Liev Dragunov's spent a lifetime plotting revenge against the Di Siones, and having Bianca's bracelet makes her perfect for his plan. Bianca must become his fake fiancée—but when Liev discovers her innocence, desire becomes sweeter than revenge...

#3458 DEMETRIOU DEMANDS HIS CHILD
Secret Heirs of Billionaires
by Kate Hewitt

Alekos Demetriou gave Iolanthe Petrakis one sinfully seductive night, never knowing that his enemy's daughter left carrying his child. Ten years later, after discovering Iolanthe's secret, Alekos declares he will legitimize his son—and that they *will* marry!

#3459 THE SHEIKH'S BABY SCANDAL
One Night With Consequences
by Carol Marinelli

Playboy sheikh Kedah Al Quasim has spent years behaving outrageously; now he must accept his royal duty and marry. His coolly beautiful assistant, Felicia Hamilton, seems the perfect distraction, but Kedah isn't prepared for the scandalous consequence: Felicia pregnant with his baby!

#3460 A RING FOR VINCENZO'S HEIR
One Night With Consequences
by Jennie Lucas

Impoverished Scarlett Ravenwood has no choice but to interrupt wealthy Vincenzo Borgia's wedding—she needs his help protecting their unborn child! To claim his heir, Vincenzo has no choice but to marry Scarlett. She suddenly has everything—except his heart!

HPCNM0816RA

#3461 TRAPPED BY VIALLI'S VOWS
Wedlocked!
by Chantelle Shaw

Waitress Marnie Clarke refuses to be Leandro Vialli's "dirty little secret," and flees, secretly pregnant. After a paternity test proves his fatherhood, Leandro must claim his heir—and when an accident steals Marnie's memories, he makes her believe they're engaged!

#3462 THE SECRET BENEATH THE VEIL
by Dani Collins

Mikolas Petrides will secure a business deal in marriage. But when he lifts the veil, he finds his intended's protective sister— Viveka Brice! With the marriage canceled, Viveka must compensate Mikolos somehow—and he's determined to make her his *mistress*.

#3463 DEFYING THE BILLIONAIRE'S COMMAND
by Michelle Conder

Dare James is furious that some woman has gotten her claws into his grandfather—but when he confronts the family doctor, she's unexpectedly attractive. Carly is no gold digger, and she can't wait to wipe the smile from Dare's handsome face!

#3464 THE MISTRESS THAT TAMED DE SANTIS
The Throne of San Felipe
by Natalie Anderson

An unexpected encounter with notorious temptress Bella Sanchez has Prince Antonio De Santis breaking his rules about women. Antonio's entrance shakes up Bella's empty life, and she can't resist a forbidden affair. But can she tame the De Santis prince?

YOU CAN FIND MORE INFORMATION ON UPCOMING HARLEQUIN® TITLES, FREE EXCERPTS AND MORE AT WWW.HARLEQUIN.COM.

HPCNM0816RB

REQUEST YOUR
FREE BOOKS!

HARLEQUIN

Presents

2 FREE NOVELS PLUS
2 FREE GIFTS!

PASSION
GUARANTEED
SEDUCTION

YES! Please send me 2 FREE Harlequin Presents® novels and my 2 FREE gifts (gifts are worth about $10). After receiving them, if I don't wish to receive any more books, I can return the shipping statement marked "cancel." If I don't cancel, I will receive 6 brand-new novels every month and be billed just $4.30 per book in the U.S. or $5.24 per book in Canada. That's a saving of at least 13% off the cover price! It's quite a bargain! Shipping and handling is just 50¢ per book in the U.S. and 75¢ per book in Canada.* I understand that accepting the 2 free books and gifts places me under no obligation to buy anything. I can always return a shipment and cancel at any time. Even if I never buy another book, the two free books and gifts are mine to keep forever.

106/306 HDN GHRP

Name	(PLEASE PRINT)	

Address		Apt. #

City	State/Prov.	Zip/Postal Code

Signature (if under 18, a parent or guardian must sign)

Mail to the **Reader Service:**
IN U.S.A.: P.O. Box 1867, Buffalo, NY 14240-1867
IN CANADA: P.O. Box 609, Fort Erie, Ontario L2A 5X3

**Are you a current subscriber to Harlequin Presents® books
and want to receive the larger-print edition?
Call 1-800-873-8635 or visit www.ReaderService.com.**

* Terms and prices subject to change without notice. Prices do not include applicable taxes. Sales tax applicable in N.Y. Canadian residents will be charged applicable taxes. Offer not valid in Quebec. This offer is limited to one order per household. Not valid for current subscribers to Harlequin Presents books. All orders subject to credit approval. Credit or debit balances in a customer's account(s) may be offset by any other outstanding balance owed by or to the customer. Please allow 4 to 6 weeks for delivery. Offer available while quantities last.

Your Privacy—The Reader Service is committed to protecting your privacy. Our Privacy Policy is available online at www.ReaderService.com or upon request from the Reader Service.

We make a portion of our mailing list available to reputable third parties that offer products we believe may interest you. If you prefer that we not exchange your name with third parties, or if you wish to clarify or modify your communication preferences, please visit us at www.ReaderService.com/consumerchoice or write to us at Reader Service Preference Service, P.O. Box 9062, Buffalo, NY 14240-9062. Include your complete name and address.

HP15

SPECIAL EXCERPT FROM

HARLEQUIN

Presents.

Harlequin Presents® has a brand-new eight-book series,
THE BILLIONAIRE'S LEGACY, *where the search for
truth and the promise of passion continue…*

*Bianca Di Sione has tried denying her obvious
attraction to Liev Dragunov and coolly rebuffs every
request to work for him. Until he finds her weakness: a
diamond bracelet she desperately needs!*

Read on for a sneak preview of
TO BLACKMAIL A DI SIONE

"If you want to stand any chance of getting your precious
bracelet back, we will become engaged." Liev said the
words so softly, all but whispering them in her ear, that to
anyone watching they would have looked like lovers. She
backed away, bumping into someone passing behind her.
She didn't apologize. She couldn't speak. All she could
think of was his cruel terms.

"I have no intention of becoming engaged and certainly
not to a man like you." She glared angrily at him, totally
shocked he could even be suggesting such a thing just to
gain entry into a world he was obviously not born into. A
world he didn't belong to.

"A man like me? A thief and a nobody?" Liev snarled
the words at her, his voice a low growl, laced with menace.

Bianca lifted her chin, not wanting to show him her
fear. "That's not what I meant and you know it."

"For your information, if I had a choice, I would not be engaged to a spoiled little rich girl such as yourself."

She smarted at his inference that she was materialistic and counted every last gem and diamond she owned. It was so far from the truth it was laughable, but right now she couldn't laugh.

"We can never be engaged. I won't do it."

"Then you will not be able to add the bracelet to your collection of trinkets." He raised his brows and a cruel smile spread over his lips.

"You purposefully bid for something I wanted just to satisfy your own greed?"

"Yes." He wasn't at all shamed by her statement—if anything he was proud of it.

"That's blackmail." She raged against him and the injustice of it all. What was she going to tell her grandfather now?

"Not blackmail, Ms. Di Sione. Business. Now do we have a deal?"

Don't miss
TO BLACKMAIL A DI SIONE by Rachael Thomas,
available September 2016 wherever
Harlequin Presents® books and ebooks are sold.

www.Harlequin.com

Copyright © 2016 by Harlequin Books S.A.

HPEXP0816R

HARLEQUIN

Presents®

*Don't miss Carol Marinelli's sensational new story,
where one night with a sheikh leads to
unexpected consequences!*

Playboy sheikh Kedah of Zazinia has loved building up his
outrageous reputation! But to claim his throne, Kedah knows
he must accept his royal duty and take a bride…

A scorching night with his poised assistant Felicia Hamilton
seems like the perfect distraction—and her cool beauty masks
a desire Kedah is hungering to ignite! But even Kedah isn't
prepared for the biggest scandal of all—when their one
night together leaves Felicia pregnant with his baby!

Don't miss

THE SHEIKH'S
BABY SCANDAL

September 2016

Stay Connected:
www.Harlequin.com
www.IHeartPresents.com

HP13465

JUST CAN'T GET ENOUGH
OF THE ALPHA MALE?
Us either!

Come join us at **I Heart Presents** to hear the latest from your favorite Harlequin Presents authors and get special behind-the-scenes secrets of the Presents team!

With access to the latest breaking news and special promotions, **I Heart Presents** is *the* destination for all things Presents. Get up close and personal with the sexy alpha heroes who make your heart beat faster and share your love of these glitzy, glamorous reads with the authors, the editors and fellow Presents fans!

www.IHeartPresents.com

HPIHEART

Whatever You're Into... Passionate Reads

Looking for more passionate reads from Harlequin®?
Fear not! Harlequin® Presents, Harlequin® Desire and
Harlequin® Blaze offer you irresistible romance stories
featuring powerful heroes.

♦HARLEQUIN *Presents*

Do you want alpha males, decadent glamour and jet-set
lifestyles? Step into the sensational, sophisticated world of
Harlequin® Presents, where sinfully tempting heroes ignite a
fierce and wickedly irresistible passion!

♦HARLEQUIN *Desire*

Harlequin® Desire novels are powerful, passionate and
provocative contemporary romances set against a backdrop of
wealth, privilege and sweeping family saga. Alpha heroes with
a soft side meet strong-willed but vulnerable heroines amid a
dramatic world of divided loyalties, high-stakes conflict and
intense emotion.

♦HARLEQUIN *Blaze*

Harlequin® Blaze stories sizzle with strong heroines and
irresistible heroes playing the game of modern love and lust.
They're fun, sexy and always steamy.

Be sure to check out our full selection of books
within each series every month!

www.Harlequin.com

HPASSION2016